BEST LESBIAN ROMANCE 2011

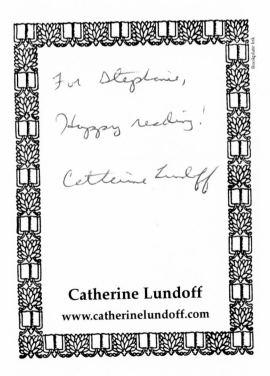

For Stephanie,

Happy reading!

Catherine Lundoff

Catherine Lundoff
www.catherinelundoff.com

BEST LESBIAN
ROMANCE
2011

EDITED BY
RADCLYFFE

CLEIS
PRESS

Published in the United States by Cleis Press, Inc., 2246 Sixth Street, Berkeley, California 94710.

Printed in the United States.
Cover design: Scott Idleman/Blink
Cover photograph: Fancy Collection/SuperStock
Text design: Frank Wiedemann
Cleis Press logo art: Juana Alicia
First Edition.
10 9 8 7 6 5 4 3 2 1

ISBN: 978-1-57344-427-9

"Lost and Found" ©2010 by Andrea Dale first appeared in *Lesbian Lust* (Cleis Press, 2010); "Boiled Peas" ©2009 by Clifford Henderson first appeared in *Romantic Interludes 2: Secrets* (Bold Strokes Books, 2009); "When Hearts Run Free" ©2009 by L. L. Raand first appeared in *Romantic Interludes 2: Secrets* (Bold Strokes Books, 2009).

Contents

INTRODUCTION

Love and romance are a classic couple, inextricably bound but subtly individual. Love is an emotion and to be *in love*, a state of being. Despite uncertainty, disillusion or loss, love seduces us again and again with the wonder of that singular connection with another heart. Once experienced, love marks us so indelibly, we continue to search, at any age, for those precious moments. And when we find them anew, the joy is still as sweet as the first time.

When reading through the scores of superb submissions for this collection, I was struck by the many ways in which we write about romance. Style, tone and voice vary every bit as much as the delicate nuances of the experiences we seek to capture with our words. These seventeen selections embody the eroticism and lyricism of love from the first blush of recognition...

> *It was the kind of first date you know will change your life forever, the kind for which "first date" is*

*much too casual to ever properly apply.... She looked
at me like she could fall for me, fall in love with me,
or maybe like she already had. She looked at me like
she wanted to know everything I had to say, to peek
inside my brain and tease out the parts I kept deliberately tucked away.*

      —"Mother Knows Best," Rachel Kramer Bussel

...to the forever embrace of shared hearts:

*"I'm not really your type, am I," she said, like she
was sad, but also resigned.*

    *I was baffled. I looked at her, her body so ripe and
luscious that her handmade bikini didn't even begin
to contain it. I felt a pain in my heart, a hairline fracture, watching this girl lose her confidence. She was
sitting there in a swimsuit she had been taught her
whole life she did not have a right to wear, and she
looked so fucking beautiful I thought I might hyperventilate or dissolve if I didn't get my hands on her
soon. How could she possibly not be aware of her
effect on me?*

    "You are exactly my type..."

      —"Rock Palace," Miel Rose

Romance encompasses a panoply of emotions: euphoria, despair,
exhilaration, the thrill of sexual awakening, the excitement of
new beginnings and the quiet contentment of the familiar. Here
in these pages is the proof that just as love never grows old,
romance never fails to touch to our hearts.

Radclyffe

HEARTS AND FLOWERS

Theda Hudson

What's romantic? Hearts and flowers? I have a heart and I think cut flowers are a crime, a waste of money, an expensive throwaway.

What's touching? It's a hand reaching out to pinch a nipple, a fingernail running down the length of a chest, tracing the pouch of a round belly.

Call me jaded. Call me jealous. I never had a lover who brought me hearts or candy or flowers. I never had a lover for a year before either. But in five days it'll be our anniversary. A year.

I'm terrible at dropping hints. Gina says not to even bother anyway, just spit it out. So I did.

"Our anniversary is on Friday," I said. "I want to celebrate."

Gina looked up from where she was settled in on my ugly brown corduroy couch, her book flopped on her lap, her dark, smoky eyes staring right at me like a banked fire on a snowy night. Her skin was pale and silky to the touch. She put lotion on every day. She'd even held me down a few times and put it on me.

Of course, then I had to wrestle her down, finally flipping her over, shrieking with laughter, tie her up and rub myself all over her, which led to other rubbing and then a nap, a glorious nap, curled up in her arms. After I'd untied her, of course. That's always the best part. Like unwrapping a present.

"Okay, Jen. What do you want to do?"

"I dunno. I never had an anniversary before." At least not this kind.

"Do you want to do dinner? Do you want to go to the Club? They're having a ladies night."

I considered. "Maybe dinner, but not the Club." We didn't meet at the Club, although we'd gone a bunch of times since she'd discovered it. We met, of all places, in the library. I was looking for CDs, she was looking for thrillers. She told me later I was more thrilling than anything she'd read all year.

No, I didn't want the spectacle and everybody's eyes in the club on us while we celebrated what had been the best year of my life. You really don't know what you're missing until she chases after you out the library doors and asks if you'd like to have coffee, a drink, anything, so she can keep looking at you.

Well. How can any red-blooded woman, American or not, say no to that?

We had coffee, then some dinner, then some pool at the neighborhood bar. She's got a good eye and she's definitely not a table ornament, as I found out to my surprise and pleasure.

"Okay," Gina said, putting her book down on her lap. "Not the Club. You want to see a movie? *Camden's Prize* is down at the Regal."

She really wanted to see that movie. It was *our* anniversary.

And she had taught me that relationships are give and take.

"Sure, we could do that."

"Okay. I'll put it on the list."

"The list?"

"I figure we'll throw a bunch of stuff out on the table and then figure out which ideas get swept off, and then we'll do what's left."

I couldn't help it. I immediately went to the night we had sushi the first time. I'd never thought watching anybody eat raw fish was sexy, but watching Gina's red mouth open to receive the pink fleshy morsel (yes, that's how I thought of it) with her dark hair framing her pale face, accenting the charcoal eye shadow she used and the eyeliner that made her eyes look huge and all knowing, I couldn't catch my breath.

I had to have her. Being practical and a bit of a masochist, I waited, watching her eat every single piece of fish. She realized I was enjoying watching her, and she gave me a real show with the last bit.

"All gone," she said, pouting those super red, luscious lips.

"Not quite, there's one piece left." I stood up, swept everything onto the floor and hoisted her up onto the table amongst the remains, smeared wasabi all over her pussy and held her down while she squirmed and screamed. I ate her until she came, explosively, adding her juice to the mess on the table and the floor.

I cleaned it up, smiling to myself, as I mopped the floor.

I smiled now, remembering it.

She recognized the smile, even if she didn't know what prompted it. She squirmed a little on the sofa.

"We could stay home," she said. "Go to bed early."

I considered. "We could. But I think it would be more interesting out here."

"I believe you," she said.

Yeah, so my apartment is a dark cave.

After a long moment, she asked, "You know what I want?"

"Twenty whacks with the bunny fur paddle?"

She blushed. She loved that paddle. Well, she loved the bunny fur. I loved the paddle. I loved the way it cracked when the leather smacked the apples of her ass. I loved the way her skin glowed red after a while. I really loved the way she wiggled around when I ran the fur over her hot flesh after I'd given her dozen good whacks.

"No, I mean yes, but that's not what I mean."

Her eyes were dark and deep and I thought I could just fall into them. And I didn't care what happened after that. Looking out of Gina's eyes couldn't be any worse than looking out of John Malkovich's eyes.

"I wanna know what this anniversary means to you."

I stared at her. What it meant to me? I drew a blank, and I just shook my head. That was the wrong thing to do. Totally, because I saw how much it hurt her, which was a revelation because even though she was hippy hoppy cute, I had never realized she might have something invested in this, in me.

"I, uh, I..."

"Never mind," she said. "It's not important."

But it was.

"Hey, Gina. It is." And it was. I had only just realized it was more important than I'd thought. More than just a year.

"But you don't know what it means to you." She lifted her book.

"I just never thought about it. The days, they just go by and I'm either at your place or you're here at mine."

"So, you just expect me to be around? As the days go by."

"Yes, no, not like that."

She closed the book and sighed. "I'm going home, Jen. It's late and I have an early morning."

"But, wait. You were going to spend the night."

"No, Jen. You just expected that I was going to spend the night." She sat up and slipped into her Danskos.

"No, Gina, really, don't go." What had I just done? What had just happened?

"Yes, Jen. I *am* going."

She walked across the room, pulled her coat off the tree and slipped her cavernous red leather purse over her arm, sliding the book into it.

"Good night, Jen." She opened the door, shut it and was gone. Without a smile or the blown kiss that I always caught.

I slumped in the ratty matching oversized armchair.

Really. What had just happened? And why did I feel so crappy about it? That was something to think about.

I texted her in the morning. *Hey! Dinner 2nite? Fuzzy Smith is on Wahoo.*

She didn't answer until late afternoon. *No, thx, 2 much 2 do.* No CU, no XO, no nothing.

Except for a huge gaping hole in my heart and a knife of pain that spitted my gut every time I thought about why I might have a hole.

What did it mean? We'd been seeing each other for a year. We hadn't said I love you, hadn't made any plans. It was fun. It was comfortable. I liked being around her. I could laugh. And she was hot and eager. I looked forward to seeing her. I liked waking up next to her.

I thought about it all day and called her after I ate a crappy dinner of microwaved chimis with a can of Miller Lite.

She answered.

"This is Gina." She always answered the phone like that. Even in this age of caller ID. She said it was a business thing. Except that usually when she recognized me, she said something like, "Hey, Lover," or "Hey, Babe."

I wanted to say, "This is a miserable person," but I thought I should put a good face on it. You know, push through.

"Hey, how you doin'?"

"I'm okay."

Well, I'm shitty. "I been thinkin'."

"Yeah?"

She wasn't going to help one bit.

"Yeah, about what you asked."

"What was that?"

I tried not to sigh into the phone. "About what this anniversary means to me."

"And what did you think?"

"That I like it when you're around. I feel good. I like waking up next to you."

"Makes me feel like an accessory. Or a toy."

What?

"No, you're more than that. You're fun and I like looking at you, at your eyes."

"Now I feel like a pinup girl or a call girl."

"I never said that. You're just twisting my words around. Why are you doing this, Gina?"

"Because you're telling me that in the entire year we've been seeing each other, you think I'm fun, good to look at, and you like waking up next to me. That's not a lot to hang anything on."

"But that's not what I meant."

"What did you mean then, Jen?"

"I, I—" How could I explain what it meant to me to see her tousled hair spread out over the Egyptian sheets we bought at that midwinter fair, sleep marks all over the side of her face from sleeping so hard, the way her warmth made me feel welcome, her smile when she woke and saw me looking at her?

"I see. I have to go."

She hung up the phone.

I sat there staring at the phone like a dumbshit.

I drank the rest of the six-pack and fell into my crappy bed, crawling across the valley in the middle and sleeping on her side. The sheets smelled like the musky lotion she used (no animals harmed in the manufacture) and her sweat.

I breathed it in until my throat swelled up with tears. A few leaked out and I passed out feeling sorry for myself.

Wednesday I was worthless at work. Not just the hangover, but trying to figure out how I could explain what this anniversary meant to me. I'd never seen anybody for more than a few months. Mostly, I just played. That's what the Club was for. I found plenty of good times there. Good scenes that made me hot and gave me fantasies that I could replay later on.

But with Gina, the fantasy was there all the time, totally real, surprising, exciting, sweet, tender. She introduced me to things I had never known, never cared about.

When I got home I looked at my apartment and realized that I hated it. The dark cave of the living room was filled with my ratty couch and chair that I'd had since right out of college. The art was just shit I bought at a garage sale so I'd have stuff on the walls.

Why was I here?

I loved Gina's place. It was a tiny studio with a twin bed and barely room for the air mattress she bought so we could sleep together there, but the room was light and filled with funky modern furniture and art from galleries she'd haunted while she was working for that interior designer a few years before she met me.

I skipped the chimis and just got drunk this time. Thursday I didn't even bother to go in. I just sat around on that ugly couch and skipped the hair of the dog. Hell, I was going straight for the entire pooch.

My life had gone from pretty fucking good to absolutely fucking awful in the course of two conversations.

"Fucking bitch, just like all the rest," I grumbled.

But that wasn't true.

This was truth: I was drunk by myself in the middle of my ugly ass living room and I hated it.

I woke up on the couch the next morning, Friday morning. My anniversary. I rolled off of it with a groan and a *thunk*.

"Yuck," I said when I got a whiff of myself.

I called in to work again and took a shower. After I got dressed in clean jeans and a T-shirt with a cardigan, I went out.

Breakfast was the first order.

I texted Gina. *Plz come over tonight. Plz. 630pm. Plz.*

I drank coffee, ate scrambled eggs, bacon and pancakes dripping in pecan syrup while I watched for her response.

It came as I was finishing the last cup.

OK. 630pm.

Well, at least she answered, and she said she'd come.

I was busy the rest of the day. I took another shower at five-thirty, got dressed in the new black brushed-denim jeans I'd bought, slipped on the new cable-knit sweater and blow-dried my hair. It cooperated nicely, one of the nicest spiky dos I'd ever managed.

I ran over my preparations one more time before the doorbell rang. And it did ring. She didn't open the door and yell, "Hey!"

At least she was here.

"Hey, Gina, come on in," I said, opening the door.

She looked great. She wore one of those knit skirts that clung to every curve, the super high-heeled boots that made me lick my lips every time I saw her in them, and a low-cut, V-neck, clingy sweater with a pear-shaped amethyst nestled just above her cleavage.

"God, you look great." I leaned in to buss her cheek. She was wearing Poison. The lotion, if I wasn't mistaken. "You smell great too."

She smiled at me, just a little, but her eyes were sharp, questioning.

"Let me take your coat." I hung it on the tree, her purse too.

"Have a seat. You want some wine? I got some Toody's pinot grigio."

She loved this wine. I hated it, too thick, trying too hard, I always thought.

"Please."

I brought two glasses, a plate of little canapés that I'd picked up from our favorite deli and the single red rose I'd bought on my errands today.

"For you."

She cocked her head and the ghost of a smile haunted her lips for just a moment. Then she was all business.

I pulled out the red paper heart with the lace edging I'd made this afternoon. "This too."

She took it, a frown line straight down the center of her forehead.

"What is it?"

"My heart."

I sat down on the easy chair and sipped the wine, managing not to make a face, then put my glass down.

"So, okay. I've been thinking really hard about your question. And what I discovered is," I paused, swallowing. This was it. If she wouldn't accept this, it was over, and I'd be left with the realization of this truth in my life and no place to put it to use, because I couldn't imagine ever finding someone like her again.

"The truth is, Gina, that I love you. And I've been selfish. All the stuff I said, it was all about me, because I never thought, I never dared to think, to imagine that there was anything else but a good time between us. I should have asked long before this, and that was wrong."

I took her hand. She let me, but never took her dark eyes off of mine. They were boring straight into me, my heart, my soul.

"You mean everything to me. I want you to know that. I'm ready to do whatever it takes to keep you in my life. I'll buy a house so we can live together. I'll buy a new bed."

She laughed then.

"What do you think?"

She flung her arms around me. "I think that was very well done. And yes, I will live with you. But *we* will buy a house and a king-sized bed. Together. And I love you too. I have from the first moment I laid eyes on you at the library."

"You did?" We would buy a house together? My heart was flipping around and I jumped up, without realizing what I was doing, pulled her up with me and swung her around. She barely missed the wineglasses, but I didn't care. I would have cleaned up anything at this point, just glad it wasn't the wreckage of my life.

"That was a very romantic anniversary," she said later, nuzzling me in the pool of musky warmth we'd made in the bed.

"Hearts and flowers," I mumbled into her neck as I fell asleep. "That's what romance is. That and recognizing it and being smart enough to give them."

MOTHER
KNOWS BEST

Rachel Kramer Bussel

I can't believe you did that to me!" I screamed into the phone
to my mother. I was fuming. If it were possible for smoke
to come out of my ears, it would have been. You'd think that
being a lesbian for the last fifteen years would have made me
off limits to my mother's meddlesome matchmaking ways, but
no, my being a dyke had only made it worse. Now she thought
the process was simplified; if she met a single girl who was at all
inclined toward women, then I was the match for her. She wasn't
concerned about the details: age, occupation, looks, never mind
butch/femme. For my mom, lesbian plus lesbian had to equal
true love. It would've been sweet, if it wasn't so infuriating.

She didn't care about things like compatibility, or personality.
She insisted that she'd met my father and known right away he
was the one, but I didn't believe her. Everyone was a little picky
about their partners, weren't they? Even if it were true, that
didn't mean she knew who was the right one for me.

It's not like I had a checklist...well, not really. But there *are* things I like in a woman, things I look for, like curves. I like a woman who's got some meat on her, whose ass I can smack, whose breasts I can get lost in sucking. I like a woman who's a little demure, who likes to have her seat pulled out for her, who likes to be doted on. No offense, but the high-powered business-women aren't really my type. I'm a painter and sculptor and spend most of my time working with my hands, getting messy. Money is messy, I guess, when you're touching it all day, and I wouldn't mind a woman who's a bartender or something like that, but the chic women in suits and pearls I sometimes run into, who look at me like I could show them a thing or two? Not interested. I'm in my late thirties and up until now have been content with mostly one-night stands. They're easier, less messy, no risk of getting my heart tied up in knots. You (or my mother) might call it cynical; I call it practical.

I like to throw her a bone once in a while—you never know who you might meet—but I'd sworn off Mom's matchmaking after the most recent fiasco. The lucky lady she'd tried to set me up with had been twenty years older than me, a wealthy divorcee who had recently realized she was more Sapphic than she'd suspected. We'd had nothing in common, even though we'd tried. That wasn't the first time. Before that, it had been a woman who screeched loudly and looked like she was trying way too hard, with '80s-style hair, too much makeup and skin-tight jeans. I like femmes, don't get me wrong, but she took the lipstick lesbian thing to a whole new level.

"Calm down, Stacy, just calm down," my mother huffed. "I'm just trying to help. Jessica was very nice when I met her at dinner with her mother, who I met at my French class. I didn't think it'd be such a big deal for her to take you to a nice dinner."

After almost a full minute of silence, I sighed. Jessica, Miss Flashdance, had been nice enough, I just wasn't attracted to her.

At all. "Fine, but don't do it again," I said, not wanting to get into the details of just how wrong things had gone on our date when Jessica had puckered up at the end of the evening and then pouted and said I was rude not to at least make out with her.

"Whoops, too late," Mom said, not sounding very contrite at all.

"What do you mean?" I asked, suspicion invading my voice.

"I mean, young lady," she said, calling up a level of properness that she only uses when she knows she's not one-hundred-percent right, "that my friend Sylvia's niece Tanya is going to call you. I think she has tickets to a concert tonight. And I saw a picture of her and I must say, even though I don't swing that way, she's hot. I think you'll like her. I'm sorry about what happened with the other date." There was a pause. "And the one before that. I just want you to be happy," she said hurriedly, as if that would make up for it. Then my mom got quiet and, I could tell from how her voice had trailed off at the end of her last sentence, somewhat contrite.

I could only imagine what kind of woman my mom would think was "hot." I shuddered, said good-bye as politely as I could and got off the phone. My mind began to wander.... I'd been reading about the power of positive thinking, and now I decided to try it. What if this Tanya really was hot? What if she was the Rubenesque goddess I'd been looking for? Even a stopped clock is right twice a day, and I wouldn't want to give up on the possible girl of my dreams before even meeting her. Plus, I could snarl at my mom, but I wouldn't have the guts to snap the head off a stranger who'd been kind enough to put up with the same horror I was currently suffering through—being set up on a date by a relative like I was a teenager, when I was actually thirty-eight.

And wouldn't you know it, but that night, I got a call from Tanya. She had a sort of Southern drawl, not something I hear every day in New York. And, god help her, she sounded sexy, maybe because she wasn't trying so hard like some of the women my mom had set me up with before. I guess you could call my type femme, just not high femme, while I'm somewhere between androgynous and soft butch. I don't go for feminine fashion, but no one's ever mistaken me for a guy. My hair is short, and I don't wear any makeup, unless SPF moisturizer counts. I wear black cowboy boots most of the time and an array of jeans and sweaters in muted colors like gray and beige, with the occasional dark purple popping up. I'm more interested in how clothes feel than how they look and often work in a paint-spattered white shirt that was once fancy and now can never be seen in public. Women check me out plenty, but once we start talking, that's usually where I run into a problem. They like what they see but not what they hear, and vice versa. They want someone snappy and witty and sophisticated, someone who's up on the latest fashion and latest gossip. That's not me at all, though I can probably tell you about the latest art exhibits.

I started to picture Tanya as she spoke, her drawl making me think of long batting eyelashes and pale cheeks, the kind that blushed easily. I couldn't be sure, though; you can't exactly ask a woman who's inviting you for beers just where she falls on the masculine/feminine scale. Somehow, though, Tanya sounded like she wouldn't be another overly made-up glamour puss. Her laugh was hearty and strong, without even a hint of a giggle.

"I'll find you, don't worry," she said, after we'd arranged to meet at Rodeo Bar to see a rockabilly band. I was glad she hadn't suggested meeting at a gay bar—though sometimes I like the boy bars, I couldn't handle an all-dyke one. I didn't want a repeat of what had happened with Jessica. As soon as she saw I wasn't that into her, she was off trying to entice another girl into dancing with her, while I nursed a beer and tried to look like I hadn't just had one of the worst dates of my life. Girl bars were out; any whiff of dyke drama and I get sucked into it so fast I barely even realize it.

We talked for about twenty minutes, and by then I was giddy in the way that I used to be back when I arranged dates for myself or made out with women after a night of drunken, sweaty dancing, then waited for them to call. Would it pan out? I resisted calling my mom to plug her for more information.

When I arrived, I tried to keep my cool; after all, Rodeo Bar is one of those scenes where it's all about keeping your cool. I liked that we were meeting in neutral territory, where we could hopefully get to know each other. I was early, or so I thought, but then I saw her. I wasn't sure how I knew, but I knew. She was knocking back a beer, her body poured into tight jeans and a skimpy little tank top that I could picture knotted beneath her breasts, her belly bared. She had a belly, and I liked that. A backside too, which I could see when she leaned forward to place her bottle on the edge of the bar and signal for another. Her honey-blonde hair was in pigtails, a cowboy hat perched on her head.

I walked over, my heart pounding.

"Hi, Stacy," she said, then gave me a cute smile.

"How'd you know it was me?"

"Umm..." She blushed a little. "Your mom gave my mom a photo of you."

"Wow," I said. "I need a drink after that."

"I'm buying," she said, bumping my hip with hers. She was perfectly at home amidst the sawdust and peanuts, even with the sparkles glinting from around her eyes. She was a femme, but she wasn't high maintenance. I checked her out while she ordered, then handed me a bottle and clinked hers to mine.

She looked to be in her midtwenties, but as we talked, I sensed she was an old soul, just one who happened to be able to dance up a storm. "Join me?" she asked at one point.

"I'd rather watch," I said. I'm not so steady on my feet and didn't want to make a fool of myself.

"Suit yourself," she shot back, then proceeded to whirl her way through two bands' sets before collapsing next to me. There was something adorably precious about her, maybe because she could dance so wildly and not care how she looked. But sitting across from me, she wiped her brow, then pulled out a mirror. "My makeup," she said with a sigh. "I should go fix it."

I leaned across the table. "No, don't. I like it like this."

"You like me sweaty?" she asked, lifting her almost-empty bottle to her brow. Seeing her lips wrapped around the head of the bottle, after the three beers I'd already had, made my thoughts swirl away from the bar and into my bedroom. I ran a thumb across her forehead.

"You think you're sweaty now, Tanya? That's nothing." My finger stayed on the edge of her cheek, and she didn't move it away. Some band was still playing, but I could barely hear them. She pulled the bottle from her lips, and I traced the wetness that was left on her mouth. She parted her lips for me, and I pressed my thumb against her tongue, then her teeth.

"Do you want to make me sweat?" she asked softly. I could see, again, the shy little girl lurking behind her eyes, the one who wasn't quite sure if she filled out those jeans as perfectly as I thought she did, the one who was maybe confident flirting with guys, cause they were easy, but found women a bit more troublesome.

This time I scooted my chair next to hers. "I want to make you scream," I said, then nuzzled my face against her neck. I don't usually move that fast, don't usually indulge in PDA, but it had been so long since I'd felt that kind of connection. Oh, I'd had girls grace my bed, my sturdy steel made-for-fucking bed that I'd spent my last major commission check on, but they had all been just that—girls. Not literally, of course—they were in their twenties, sometimes their thirties—but none had affected me like she had. I couldn't even say exactly what it was she'd done to wrap me around her little finger so fast, but Tanya had done it. I was the one breathing heavily as I rested my head against her skin, soaked in her scent of sweat and strawberry and beer.

She looked back at me then, her face open, bared to me in a way most city girls never dare. I wondered for a second if she'd lose that look down the road, learn to mask it with a big city veneer. Then a smile peeked out, a different one than what she'd offered earlier, more tentative. She wasn't on the prowl; she didn't have to be, because she'd already caught me, and I her.

This time, I did pull her up to dance—well, really I fondled her ass and tried to stay out of the way of the couples whirling around us. We lasted for a few songs before I had to take her home. By then it was a question of need, and it had nothing to do with my mother, nothing to do with the way men and women in the room stared at her and everything to do with the way Tanya stared at me, asking me with her eyes to give her something she desperately needed.

It was the kind of first date you know will change your life forever, the kind for which "first date" is much too casual to ever properly apply. We took a cab back to my place in Brooklyn, and I was grateful for perhaps the first time that I'd carved out a separate studio space and bedroom. For many years they'd been one and the same, with me sleeping on a cot next to my art, my true love. Maybe I was finally ready to let someone else in, truly in. Before I could make a move to get Tanya's clothes off, she insisted on a tour. The other girls had only given the most cursory of glances to my work, letting me know what they really wanted was in my pants. Tanya's eyes told me she wanted everything. My heart, my art, my pussy.

I reached beneath her shirt, cupping that belly, pinching it, holding it, as I showed her my favorite pieces, even my latest in-progress sculpture, one I wasn't quite sure what it would become. She didn't just listen but asked questions, probed more deeply than anyone had before. Whereas when we'd been dancing all I'd wanted was to get her clothes off, to make her scream and sweat and let me know she wanted me, now I wanted more than just to get her off. I wanted to light up her mind as well as her pussy, and she seemed to want both as well.

I told her I'd explain my art if she stripped for me. We moved to the bedroom, and I told her things I'd never told anyone before, not since my art school days. It sounds strange, perhaps, that instead of her shimmying to a seductive song, it was my soul that got bared. Well, her body did too. She took her clothes off languorously, but I was focused on her eyes. Her blue eyes and her naturally pink lips, her face, traces of glitter still on it, her look so open, so eager. There was still passion simmering between us, but there was something more. She looked at me like she could fall for me, fall in love with me, or maybe like she already had. She looked at me like she wanted to know every-thing I had to say, to peek inside my brain and tease out the parts I kept deliberately tucked away.

When she again brought her lips down for a kiss, I couldn't believe how much I'd told her. My heart was pounding as we kissed, long and slow, kisses that weren't like the ones before at the bar, weren't searching for anything beyond their own boundaries. We knew we wanted each other and would have each other. For that night, the knowing was enough.

Another first. I'd never brought a woman home before and not fucked her, but for some reason, with Tanya I was content to simply soak up her beauty. I played with her nipples, sucking them fiercely, frantically. I wanted to fuck her, but I also wanted to wait. Instead, I cast her, immortalized her.

She sat for me as I painted her beautiful arms, her proud breasts, the curves of her waist and ass, her belly, with plaster of paris, and she sat for me as it hardened. When I peeled it off and set the cast down, I knew she'd be mine, one way or another, forever.

Luckily Tanya stuck around, and my mom even had the honor of giving me away, though she snuck in a triumphant "I told you so" before I walked down the aisle. I couldn't be mad, and Tanya is now my wife, my muse, my love, and soon she will be the mother of our child. She was worth every second I waited for her.

TWELFTH
NIGHT

Catherine Lundoff

If music be the food of love, play on!" Tasha threw her arms wide as she gleefully quoted from our upcoming production of Shakespeare's *Twelfth Night*. She collapsed into one of the scruffy armchairs in the changing room all the members of the Bardic Women's Theater Company shared. Lucky us—or me, at least, at the moment.

Tasha was in costume as Orsino, Duke of Illyria, and she had a lovely pair of legs in tights. It didn't stop there though; the rest of her was quite easy on the eyes and the fantasy life too, right up to her big brown eyes and slightly upturned nose. And the smile that lit up the theater.

I sat in one of the other chairs watching her covertly and hoping that no one else would notice that I was in crush, and I had it bad. I should get so lucky.

Sara kicked my leg from the opposite seat. "Yo, BJ, you paying attention? Of course not. Why would we be paying attention to running through our lines when opening night is only three days away?"

I stuck my tongue out at her. "I can't help it if your Countess Olivia just isn't doing it for me. Try throwing in a gesture or two or maybe showing some skin."

"And suddenly you're an expert on acting? You only got Viola's part because..."

I stared at her, daring her to finally say what everyone else was thinking. The room got very quiet. But I could see Sara change her mind an instant later, and she finished with something she'd clearly made up on the spot.

"You're so believable as a femme in drag!" She was standing now, glaring down at me.

This was pretty much out of left field, so I just stared up at her for a minute while I thought about it. Granted, I had the longest hair in the company and the longest nails, but that was the celibacy talking, not femme preference. It wasn't like I even particularly wanted the role, though I thought I'd earned it. But at least Sara hadn't said it was because our director, Nadine, had been trying to get into my tights ever since her ex dumped her a few months back.

From time to time, I had nearly said yes, but Nadine was so...not Tasha. Plus it would have been really, really messy on so many levels. Nadine added a whole new dimension to the term "drama queen." My expression must've changed because Sara suddenly went bright red and backed away. Before I could ask what her problem was, I got interrupted.

"Hello, my dears!" Nadine bounced in with a cheery trill, and we all sat up and got very alert. As a rule, she wasn't much of a triller. "Gather round, gather round." She was holding up a piece of paper and grinning at us in a positively evil way.

We gathered, somewhat reluctantly. Sara elbowed me, I elbowed her back. Tasha glanced our way and rolled her eyes. It was my turn to blush.

Nadine paused for dramatic effect, one eyebrow arching upward as she looked over. I tried to look contrite while she waved the piece of paper in her hand like a flag. "Well, my dears, not that you deserve it, but it seems that Grace Smythe is interested in seeing our little production! She'll be here on opening night."

All fourteen of us gaped at her for minute or so. Grace Smythe was one of the biggest critics in the country for women's theater so this was huge. Most of the time, we were lucky to get a paragraph on the local "LGBT Things to Do Calendar." If Grace Smythe liked us, on the other hand, we could play to full houses, maybe even go on tour. Not like New York or L.A. or anything crazy like that, but maybe Pride somewhere big enough that we hadn't dated more than 75 percent of our audience.

Looking around, I could see everyone else thinking the same thing. Except Tasha. Her face had lit up like a candle, and she was wearing an expression that suggested that she was thinking about something bigger than our dating prospects. All of a sudden, my stomach felt like it had lead weights in it. There was no reason that she shouldn't think big: she had a real theater background, and she was good, better than me even. She could move on and up. And away.

Nadine sensed weakness and sidled up to me, resting her hand on my shoulder. She ignored my small flinch. "So," she continued, still trilling a bit, "I know that you'll all want this opening night to be our very best, which means all-day rehearsals. And, of course, you will all know your lines and entrances without prompting by tomorrow." There were two or three groans, one of which might have been from me. "Now let's get to it," Nadine finished as if she hadn't heard a thing. She squeezed the back of my neck, then let go and walked away, heading purposefully for Tasha.

"What do you think she gets out of it?" Sara murmured.

"I dunno. Power. Glory. The eternal gratitude of the Immortal Smythe." I watched Tasha give Nadine the full power of her most charismatic smile and sighed again. All I knew was that I wasn't going to get anything out of it: I was a decent actor when I was on, but I didn't have the chops for even off-off-Broadway. Not like Tasha. I shoved the growing ball of insecurity down into my gut where I thought I could ignore it for a while. "Well, whatever it is, Nadine's going to take it out on us if we blow it, so I suggest we get back to rehearsing. I've got to leave for work soon."

Sara didn't move out of the way when I starting walking, so of course I bumped into her. She caught my arms when I staggered, and our eyes met from just a bit too close. There was a look in her eyes that made me feel pretty weird. I mean, we'd known each other since freshman year. She was my best friend, not someone I'd think about that way. My mouth went dry and I tried to step back.

"Hey, wake up in there. What is it with you tonight anyway? I just wanted to say that I was kidding before. You're a great Viola." Sara looked earnest and that extra something, whatever it was, disappeared like I'd imagined it.

"Yeah, I know. Goof." I nudged her and grabbed my dress for the first scene, the one right after the shipwreck. My tunic and tights for my trouser role scenes were already hanging on the rack. You had to love *Twelfth Night:* girl disguised as boy meets boy who loves other girl who falls in love with girl disguised as boy. In short, gender-play, subtext and the chance to flirt while showing your legs off. It always made me wonder if Shakespeare spent more time with Marlowe than the history books suggested.

Everything went to hell after that. Tasha was the exception, but even she seemed distracted. Right after Chantay flubbed her lines for the third time, Nadine exploded. After twenty minutes of being told that we were completely devoid of talent, something clicked in my head. Why was I doing this at all if I wasn't going anywhere with it? I surprised myself by turning and walking out without a word.

I could feel them all staring after me, mouths open. Truthfully, I would have been doing the same thing if it had been anyone else walking out. I wasn't sure where I found the guts to do it either. Of course, my manager at the coffee shop had said she'd fire me if I kept being late for my shift, and I did need to pay rent. At least I could be a terrific barista even if I couldn't act professionally, though that dream was dying hard.

Sara and Tasha caught up with me about a block away from the theater. "BJ!" Sara's voice was insistent behind me, but it was Tasha who reached out and grabbed my arm to stop me. My stomach did a few leisurely flips, while I wondered how they'd found the nerve to follow me. Nadine must've called a break.

I met Sara's eyes and cringed. I'd never seen her look so upset. Her tone matched her expression. "What the hell are you doing? You can't walk out on us like this."

I wondered how long there'd been an "us" to walk out on. Sara had never cared much about Bardic Women. She threatened to quit at the end of every season when the company shrank back down to Nadine, the two of us, and whoever couldn't get an internship somewhere else. I wondered why she stayed, but it was a thought I kept to myself for the moment. "I have to get to work." I hated how whiney I sounded, but there didn't seem to be much I could do about it.

"Fair enough, but then say that. We thought you were bailing, like, forever." Tasha raised an eyebrow. "It'll be hard to pull this show off without a Viola, and I don't know if I'm up for being a last minute understudy."

Ah, yes, now I knew why she was here. Tasha's expression was pure innocence, but I couldn't help seeing something calculating swimming just below the surface. She hadn't followed me because she suddenly cared. She just wanted to know if I was coming back. Truthfully, Viola probably *should* have been Tasha's, but I had seniority, so I got the star part. Of course, giving her Viola now just might give me a shot with her.

Suddenly I wasn't so sure that I wanted to do that. Sara was looking from Tasha to me and what I could see of her expression from the corner of my eye was weirdly blank. "Oh, yeah. I'd forgotten that Nadine made you the understudy for Viola." I kept my tone as casual as I could. Here went nothing. "Look, I've got to get going. I'll be back tomorrow to talk to Nadine, but I'm fine if you rehearse the part today."

"What?" They both spoke at once.

I didn't look at Sara when I said it; something told me that whatever expression she was wearing, I didn't want to see it just yet.

Tasha hesitated just long enough to give the impression that she had her doubts about this. I tried not to hold my breath. If this got me anywhere with her, I'd be "patience on a monument, smiling at grief," as Viola put it. It would be worth it. I hoped.

Tasha suddenly threw her arms around me and gave me a huge hug. "Thank you!" She stepped back, cheeks glowing with excitement, managing to look as though her reaction was spontaneous. "I'll talk to Nadine and explain about you having to go to work and me filling in. See you tomorrow, BJ!" She took off toward the theater, leaving Sara and me staring after her.

Sara exhaled like she too had been holding her breath. "I'll walk you to work. I need a break from Nadine anyway." She headed toward the coffee shop and I trailed after her, my mood still yo-yoing up and down. "So what was that?"

I waited to be told that I was a complete idiot. When that didn't happen, I glanced sidelong at Sara. She was frowning down at her high-tops, not even looking my way. Honestly, I wondered if I was being an idiot, too. Tasha seemed grateful right now and this grand gesture might get me somewhere with her for a little while, but was that all I wanted? I decided to deflect my personal angst. "You ever think about dating anyone in the company?"

Sara jumped about a foot and stared at me with enormous hazel eyes. "Why? What have you heard?"

Oooh, I'd struck a nerve. I gave her my best swarmy grin. "It's the talk of the changing room." She kept staring at me until I felt guilty. "Okay, I made that part up. Not sure what's actually going on, but I was thinking that you and Nadine had a lot in common."

Sara went bright red and turned away. "And it's just coincidental that if she was chasing me, she'd leave you alone? Of course not. This is all about my best interests, right, old pal? After all, Nadine has a lot to offer: starring parts in the plays, being just one small element." Her voice sounded like she was off the planet somewhere and not in a good way.

"Ouch. I didn't sleep with her to get Viola and you know it. And you do have some things in common: grad school, knitting, all that stuff. Anyway, it's not like your romantic horizons look any brighter than mine right now." I could feel her stiffen and realized that I probably should have left that last part off.

Sara spun around, one finger pointed at my nose. "Don't you dare try and unload your cast-off crushes on me, BJ Drake! I know full well that you strung Nadine along for months before Tasha came along and she suddenly got inconvenient. What was it, was she a bit too old or maybe just not hip enough for you? You're a real piece of work, you know that? As of right now, I'm officially giving up on you!" She was nearly hyperventilating when I caught her hand and pulled it down away from my face. We stared at each other for a second too long, then she yanked her arm free and took off, back toward the theater.

What the hell? I stared after her, my insides churning. I thought about going after her, but then I really would be late and probably fired. Instead I went to work, my head swimming with the different women in my life. I hadn't led Nadine on, had I? I admitted that I had stopped thinking about her six months back when Tasha showed up. But that was just because Tasha was gorgeous and we had a shared love of acting. And…I'm sure there was something else if I just thought about it. Besides, since when did Sara care? I was baffled.

The next day, I was back at the theater, groggy but ready to make decisions. I'd spent part of my sleepless night memorizing Duke Orsino, since I was pretty sure that was the way the wind was blowing. The question was whether or not Nadine would go for it.

As luck would have it, she was waiting for me when I got there. "What's this about you not wanting to play Viola?" Her voice was set to non-trill, which didn't come as too much of a surprise.

I waded in. "Let's face it, Tasha's a better fit for the part than I am. I've got a lot of Orsino ready to go, if that helps."

"Maybe I don't think Tasha's right for this role. Does it ever occur to you that I might actually know what I'm doing?" Nadine scowled at me. "Are you just going to blow Viola's part if I insist that you play it?"

Man, first Sara, now Nadine. "Why the hell is everyone so down on me all of a sudden? You want to impress Smythe;

maybe I'm not the one to do it." I crossed my arms, glaring back at Nadine. I scared myself a little when I realized that I actually meant it. That was really going to hurt when I had time to think about it.

We were still having a stare down when Tasha showed up. "Hi there. What are you two up to?"

Nadine turned a momentarily icy look her way. Tasha's face froze, which lasted right up until Nadine started talking again. "I haven't made any decisions about changes in casting, if that's what you mean."

Tasha flinched slightly. "Sorry! I didn't mean anything, really." Her eyes darted to mine, their expression pleading. This should be good for at least coffee after rehearsal. I made myself not smile as I cleared my throat to make the big speech I'd thought up on my way in.

Nadine held up a hand and frowned. "All right. I think we'll try it today with Tasha as Viola and see how it goes. I don't like it, and you switch back again. No arguments. Do I make myself clear?"

Tasha nodded like a bobblehead while I took the more laid-back single nod approach. That was when the rest of the company started to trickle in, fortunately, so we went off to get into costume. "How pissed off is she?" Tasha muttered softly at me as we grabbed our respective pairs of tights.

"Not thrilled. But that's all right. I'm sure we'll wow her." I grinned at Tasha like I meant it and waited for the pleasant internal flip of my belly to tell me that my crush was still going strong. When that didn't show up, I started to get worried but decided to make my move anyway. "So after rehearsal..."

But Sara was frowning at me over Tasha's head, so instead I switched to, "Hi, Countess. How's tricks?" At least I could pretend everything was normal.

Sara raised an eyebrow. "Tricks? I might ask you the same thing. Are we Viola today or someone else? Or have we switched plays and are now doing *The Tempest?*"

Tasha snorted. "*Henry V.*"

"I was going to say *Richard III*. The answer to your snarkily phrased question is that, yes, Nadine said we could try switching roles for today." I finished tugging on Orsino's doublet and shoes before bowing low in Sara's general direction. "Until later, fair lady." She rolled her eyes and we left to go onstage.

My first scene with Tasha was awkward, filled with missed lines and flubbed cues and all the other flotsam and jetsam of a poorly rehearsed production. Then she hit her stride. By the time she had her first scene with Sara as the Countess, she was smoking up the stage. Sara was stiff, reluctant to respond, but too much of an actor herself not to. By the time they were done, I could believe that the Countess was falling in love with Viola.

It was a surprisingly unpleasant feeling. I was being upstaged. It got worse when I saw Sara giggling offstage with Tasha. Nadine walked past me as I watched them. "Do better, or else we'll have you playing Sir Andrew Aguecheek," was all she said. That got me sufficiently pissed off, seeing as Sir Andrew's an idiot, that I went into the alleyway and rehearsed my next scene until I hardly needed to look at the page.

Then I stomped back in and was the best Duke Orsino I could be for the rest of rehearsal. Nadine gave us all a nod of approval as we finished up the last scene, the one in which everyone finds their true love and everything is set right. I still had my arm around Tasha when we finished our bows: I had very nearly forgotten that the Duke wins her in the end. That was something, at least.

She shrugged loose from my arm the minute we finished, bolting over to Nadine like she had wings. I watched her go and felt some of the smitten run out of me like I'd sprung a leak. "You know," Sara said thoughtfully from somewhere near my right ear, "she's starting to grow on me."

"Because she's after my part and she's likely to get it? Or because she's oblivious to my charms?" I crossed my arms and scowled.

"Both. She's giving you some competition, and frankly, you needed it." Sara was studying her nails like they were going to do something interesting.

"Indeed?" I stalked away, then slowed down and tried to stroll toward Tasha and Nadine like I hadn't a care in the world. I couldn't help but notice that Nadine wasn't glaring at Tasha anymore.

In fact, she turned around as I walked up and threw her arm around my shoulders like we were the best of buddies. "I take it back, BJ dear. You were right. I think Grace might really go for this." She was glowing and eyeing Tasha in a speculative way that was quite familiar.

I felt like I'd been punched in the gut. Was the whole world topsy-turvy today or what? Tasha eyed Nadine right back and switched the wattage on her smile just a bit higher. I was looking at the new Viola, that much was clear. "Congratulations," I muttered through clenched teeth.

Tasha barely glanced at me. "I've got tons of rehearsing to do. Nadine, do you think you'll have time to help me go over my lines again tonight? I want to make sure I've got everything perfect."

Nadine's arm vanished from my shoulders like smoke. "Certainly, dear. Let me just finish up with the rest of the cast." *Dear?* I was "dear." She glanced at me. "Decent Orsino, BJ, but you need to pitch your voice a bit farther to make sure that you're audible in the back." She patted my arm and walked off like I was yesterday's news.

I was standing there with my mouth open when Sara walked up. Gently, she lifted my lower jaw until my lips closed and I jerked my head away. "I suppose you think this is pretty funny."

"Nope." She stopped as if thinking about it. "Well, maybe a little. You can't say you didn't have some of this coming. You played one too many games this time around." I was staring moodily off into space, determined that I wasn't going to respond. "I'll call you later, if I get back at a reasonable hour."

Startled, I gave her a long look: makeup, black leather boots, green silk shirt with a plunging neckline. She looked hot. Really hot. "You've got a date!" I said, realizing that it sounded like an accusation.

She pursed glossy lips at me in an air kiss and left me standing there like an idiot in a doublet and tights while the lights went out around me. Now what? I changed into my street clothes, cursing Nadine and Tasha and *Twelfth Night* under my breath the whole time. I couldn't really blame Sara, seeing as it was my dumb idea in the first place.

I did wonder who she was going out with tonight, though. Funny that she hadn't mentioned that there was anyone she was interested in. I wondered if she was cuter than me, whoever she was. Now where had that come from? An idea bubbled up from my little brain as I headed outside to go to my lonely little efficiency. I dismissed it firmly....

Only to have it work its way back up to the surface later on that evening when I was eating my leftovers in front of the TV and fending off the cats. Clearly, I was getting nowhere with Tasha and that wasn't going to change. So I was back to contemplating all the other constants in my life. It was a short list. I thought I knew who'd be left standing at Bardic Women after this production was over, for instance. But this time, I wondered if the list would include me.

That was when it occurred to me to wonder why Sara stuck around, show after show. She wanted to study and teach drama, not actually perform. Then I remembered how I thought she'd looked at me yesterday. Oh. So this was what a facepalm moment looked like from the inside.

The mere thought of Sara came with an unexpected bunch of fluttery feelings and a lengthy screech from the depths of whatever common sense I still possessed. We'd been friends forever. And that was it: just friends. Anything I said could destroy that. Maybe I should just do the smart thing and chicken out. Everything could go on the way it always had.

I managed to fall asleep eventually even though I still had no idea what, if anything, I was going to do tomorrow. The last thing I remembered thinking was that Duke Orsino gets Viola, not Olivia; Olivia has to settle for Viola's brother Sebastian. Clearly this wasn't going to work out: it was a sign.

My brain looped around like this through my morning shift. By the time I hit the theater, I had managed to forget that today was dress rehearsal but had succeeded in developing a whole new obsession, namely not thinking about Sara that way. Go me.

Not being psychic, she chose the moment I was thinking about not thinking about her to wander up to me at the changing tables. "Sorry I didn't call last night. I got in a bit late." She smiled in a purely evil, smug with unspoken implications, sort of way.

I felt my ears go crimson. "It's okay. I was busy myself."

"Indeed? Don't tell me Ms. Tasha changed her mind after all?" She raised an eyebrow but I thought I could detect some anxiety in her eyes. Or at least I hoped that I could.

"'Orsino's mistress and his fancy's queen?' Alas, no." I

wondered what to say next, but only for about two seconds. That's the best part about being an actor, never being at a loss for words. "Just how good was this date? Anyone I know?"

Sara gave me a sidelong devilish grin, and the butterflies in my stomach did a slow tango. "Jealous much?"

"Yes." The word popped out of my mouth before I could stop it and hung there in the air between us until I could've sworn that it was flickering like neon. Sara stared at me while I hunted for the words that would make it all a joke that we could laugh off. She reached out and pressed her finger to my lips to stop whatever I was going to say.

"It wasn't that great. Wait until tomorrow night to say whatever you're going to say. I want to see if you still mean it then." And she bolted for her costume, which I might have taken personally had I not heard Nadine yelling for us to get ready at the same moment.

That night, I was Orsino, my frustrated love for Olivia filling the stage in every scene I had. By the end of dress rehearsal, even Tasha was looking at me speculatively. Nadine walked up and gave me a one-armed hug. "I don't know what's gotten into you, but I like it."

"Me too." Sara gave me a smile that lit up the theater, brighter than any of Tasha's had ever been. But we stopped it there, and each went home alone. Tomorrow, we'd do our best and see what it looked like on the other side.

I'd love to say that the opening night went without a hitch, but then I'd be lying for no good reason. I couldn't speak for anyone else, but I got almost no sleep so my Orsino was off to a rocky start. I wasn't the only one: Sara tripped on her skirts, a few of the others forgot one or two of their lines. But once we all got going, it was our best show ever. With one exception. Tasha blew her lines completely, not once but twice, as well as part of an entrance. We covered where we could, but there was no way Smythe didn't notice it.

The weird thing was that Tasha didn't seem too unhappy about it. Not pleased, mind you, but not frantically unhappy either. By Act Three, she was back to being amazing, almost like her flubs had been staged. I was baffled but I waited until the end to ask. I had more important things on my mind, after all.

Nadine gave us one anguished look at the end, then bolted up a few rows to talk to a distinguished-looking woman with gray hair and black-framed glasses. She was frowning over a notebook, which didn't bode well. I glanced sidelong at Tasha, releasing my arm from her waist before she could pull away. "What happened?"

Tasha looked over at Nadine and gave a real smile. "I found something I wanted more, at least for now." She gave me a side-long look. "How about you?"

Sara walked up just then and I reached for her hand. She lit up like a Christmas tree and pulled me into her to give me a slow, deep, long-delayed kiss. When we came up for air, I muttered, "Yep."

But Tasha was already offstage, heading for Nadine and Grace Smythe. I saw her squeeze Nadine's hand and I smiled. "All's well that ends well."

"Wrong play." Sara hugged me close and sighed happily. "Though better that than *Romeo and Juliet.*"

I spun her around and borrowed a few more lines from the Bard. "But now our play is done, and I'll strive to please you every day!"

"Until next season," Sara wrinkled up her nose, but she didn't sound too unhappy.

"For all the seasons yet to come." I leaned down and kissed her again, and we went to change into our street clothes.

BOILED PEAS

Clifford Henderson

Penny's heart had been trampled so many times she often thought of it as raw hamburger. Or an overripe persimmon pecked to death by birds and then dropped—*splat!*—from a tree.

True, she was overly sensitive. Or that's what her mom always said when she came to visit, which she just had. And although her mom lived 4,915 miles away, her words had a way of sticking around after she left. They'd wrap around Penny like an itchy blanket. "You ask too much. Want too much. Quit looking for the pea, princess." The pea line was her mom's favorite.

Penny ripped open the bag of frozen Safeway peas and let them tumble into the boiling water. It was her twenty-fourth birthday, and she was celebrating with a bottle of Veuve Clicquot and boiled peas. She wanted to accept her fate. Swallow it down. The too-picky princess who could never be satisfied.

Her cat Screech looked up from his nest of pillows on the

couch. He was always interested when she was in the kitchen.

"Believe me, you wouldn't like this," Penny said to him, then went back to studying the dancing peas as if they were tea leaves.

It was silly really, to be obsessing over her mother's words this way. She was twenty-four now and had a good job as an intern at the Natural History Museum. So why couldn't she be more confident, like her friend Kai?

Kai was a sculptor who taught yoga at a local spa to pay the bills and didn't even want to fall in love. "Why would I want someone to muck up my perfect life?" she'd said to Penny just the other day. But it was different for Kai. Kai enjoyed one-night lovers.

Penny broke up a clump of frozen peas with a spoon while picturing Kai and someone equally flexible contorting them-selves into Kama Sutra–like poses, and thought to herself, *I could never do that with someone I'd just met.*

It took Penny time to trust a person. She needed to feel loved.

She popped the cork on her bottle of Veuve Clicquot and held it over the sink to keep the froth from getting on the floor. *What a waste,* she thought as she licked the expensive cham-pagne from her fingers. She'd given up a haircut to afford it. Pouring the champagne into one of a pair of etched champagne glasses she'd given as a Valentine's gift to Phoenix, her last, and longest, love, she thought how sure she'd been that Phoenix would be her forever. They'd even moved in together.

Then Phoenix's mentally unbalanced brother showed up, and Phoenix told him he could stay until he worked something else out. It was pleasant at first. The three of them would have dinner together, and once they'd all gone to bed, she and Phoenix would talk about how well he seemed to be doing. Then he began to leave raw egg in the pockets of Penny's jackets. She'd reach in and her fingers would be covered in slime. She asked Phoenix if maybe this wasn't a bad sign, but all Phoenix said was she'd talk to him. When he locked himself out and smashed the plateglass window to gain entry, Penny was almost relieved. Surely now Phoenix would have to ask him to leave. But Phoenix hadn't seen it that way. "He was locked out, Penny. What was he supposed to do? I'll talk to his doctor about adjusting his medication."

"But if he doesn't take his medication, which he doesn't, what difference will it make?"

"Give him a chance!" Phoenix yelled back. And so Penny had. Until he came brandishing the sewing scissors at the two of them, at which point Phoenix finally admitted his being around was a problem. But by then it was too late. Penny's trust was gone.

Before that there was her second-longest relationship, Mandy, who insisted her Great Dane sleep with them even though the flea-infested giant kept pushing Penny out of bed.

Maybe she did ask too much.

She dipped a spoon into the pot of peas, scooped one up, blew on it, almost placed it on her tongue, then let it plop back into the boiling water. She planned to eat a whole bowl full, every last one. Even if she did despise peas. She needed to accept the truth about herself. She'd never be truly happy. Never.

She took a sip of Veuve Clicquot to wash the pea flavor from her mouth, then began singing in her head, *Happy Birthday to me. Happy Birthday to me. Happy Birthday dear—*

There was a knock at the door. She glanced at the clock. No one ever dropped by unannounced. The only apartment she'd been able to afford was too far away from the rest of her friends.

She tucked her pink fluffy robe around her, cinched it in so it wouldn't accidentally slip open and went to peer out the peephole. Screech, who'd also been startled by the knock, glared at the door as if by sheer will he could make it go transparent and be able to see through to the other side.

The back of someone's head was all Penny could see. Someone who had a lovely, long, black braid. No, two braids, one right on top of the other. Penny set the chain and cracked open the door. "Can I help you?"

The someone with the long, black braids turned around, revealing a sassy-looking dyke wearing a low-slung tool belt weighted down by a hammer, a tape measure, a few screwdrivers and a bunch of other tools. In her hand was a toolbox decorated with vintage decals. She was tanned, with lean muscles, and her mouth tipped up to one side. Her T-shirt said: GIRL SCOUT GONE BAD.

"Sorry it's so late. But you contacted management about a flickering light?"

Which Penny had, almost two weeks ago. She scrutinized the woman. How old was she? Penny decided they were about the same age. "Um. Yes, I did. I most certainly did. Are you the new handyman—er, woman— they told us about?"

"I guess you could call me that, although I'd prefer if you'd call me Lil. I hope it's okay I just came over without you returning my call, but—"

"You called?"

"Yeah."

Penny glanced at her machine. Sure enough, it was blinking. "I must have been in the shower."

"If it's more convenient for me to come back…"

"No. No. This is fine."

"Again, sorry about being so late, but Mrs. Dunbar's drain

in 6B was way clogged. Apparently she washes her Pomeranian in the sink."

There was a pause in the conversation, and Penny realized they were still standing on opposite sides of the door with a chain lock between them. "I guess I should let you in then."

"Only if it's convenient. Like I said in my message. I've got a slot on Thursday I could plug you into."

"Oh, please. You're here. Why don't you just plug me now— I mean, in! Plug me in!" Blood flooded Penny's cheeks. "I can't believe I just said that! I meant, you're here, we might as well get on with it. You know, fix the light."

Lil smiled, her leprechaun-green eyes flashing mischief, but Penny refused to be moved. She was not about to get sucked into another disappointment. No way.

"My name's Penny."

"So what say you let me in then, Penny?"

Penny thought for a moment, then unlatched the lock. She did need her light fixed. As she opened the door, she became ultraaware of how she must appear. It was a Friday night, and here she was hanging around her apartment in her robe and holding a glass of champagne. Her hair was a mess. "It's…it's my birthday and I was kind of…celebrating."

Lil looked past her. "By yourself?"

Penny nodded toward Screech who was cleaning his butt. "He may not look it now, but he's quite the party animal."

Lil set her toolbox on the floor and crouched down to massage Screech's chin. "Hey, bud, you gonna help Miss Penny celebrate?" Screech rubbed up against her hand. "He's a real lover."

Surprised to see her usually suspicious cat taking to Lil so easily, Penny said, "Yeah, he is."

After one final stroke down Screech's back, Lil stood. "So why don't you show me that light?"

"Oh, right. It's in the bedroom."

As Penny led Lil down the hall to the bedroom she couldn't stop jabbering. "It's not that big of a thing, really. I mean it still turns on. But about a month ago it just sort of started to strobe." She stepped into the bedroom and switched on the flickering light.

Lil placed her toolbox on the floor and looked up at the light. "I can't believe it took you two weeks to call. This would annoy the hell out of me."

"Well, I'd just had a problem with my dishwasher leaking, so it felt funny to call again in the same month."

Lil flicked the switch on, then off, then on again. "No one should have to put up with a light like this."

Penny, suddenly overly warm and horribly self-conscious, blurted, "Especially an epileptic," and then to her horror, began laughing so hard she snorted.

Lil looked away from the light fixture. "Hey, are you all right? You seem kind of keyed up."

"I'm fine," Penny said, pinching the top of her nose to regain composure. "I think it's this birthday thing. It's got me kind of...I don't know...emotional."

Lil sat on the edge of the bed and began unlacing her boots. "So, if you don't mind me asking, how old are you?"

Why was this complete stranger taking off her boots—on *her* bed? Then Penny realized Lil didn't want to get the bed dirty when she stood on it. "Twenty-four," she said, admiring the cleanliness of Lil's socks.

Lil unscrewed the bulb. "Do you have a new one we could try?"

"In the hall closet," Penny said and went to retrieve it. She couldn't stop thinking how considerate it was that Lil had taken off her boots to stand on the bed. Considerate and oddly intimate.

"Here's a new bulb."

Lil screwed it in. The flicker was still there. "I'm going to need to turn off your breaker."

"It's in the—"

"Closet. I know. It's the same for all the apartments."

It was right then Penny smelled the peas. "Crap!"

"What?"

"My peas are probably dead by now."

"Your peas?"

"Long story," Penny said as she bolted for the kitchen.

The water was all gone and it stunk. She turned off the stove and poked at the bloated peas on top; those underneath were black. She sighed. Of course she'd still eat them, or at least skim a few off the top. She had to. Because while princesses in fairy tales always got their wish and lived happily ever after, those in real life were invariably disappointed. And tonight was about accepting that—fully.

"It's about to go dark," Lil called from the hall. "Same breaker for the bedroom and the living room."

"Do you need me to hold a flashlight for you?"

"Naw. I got a headlamp. You just sit back and enjoy your birthday."

Penny took the pot of peas and bottle of champagne into the living room. She lit a candle. Screech stepped lightly onto her lap. She scratched behind his ear. "Thanks for coming to my party."

The sounds of Lil futzing around in the bedroom made her feel secure. She'd always liked people who could fix things.

She drained her glass and poured another, then another. There was no use rushing this concession to her mother. She had all night. And the peas sure weren't going anywhere. She peered into the pot, scooped out a spoonful of green mush and sniffed it.

A girl like her would never be satisfied. Her mother was right. She asked too much—was too sensitive. She held the spoonful up, shut her eyes and prepared to shove the spoonful of disgusting peas into her mouth.

"Just wanted you to know I'm about to turn the breakers back on."

Penny opened her eyes and was dazzled by the spotlight of Lil's headlamp. She blinked a couple of times, the spoon suspended in front of her mouth.

"If you don't mind my asking, what are you doing?" Lil asked.

"Me?"

Lil looked over her shoulder. "Is there anyone else here I should know about?"

Penny let the spoon drop into the pot and blinked back tears. She was buzzed, no two ways about it. "Nothing. I was just about to eat my fate."

"Is that what's so stinky?"

"You've no idea," Penny said. Then something about being in the spotlight while seriously smashed on champagne uncorked Penny's bottled-up fears, and before she knew it she was spilling out all over the place, telling Lil about never being able to be happy, and the raw eggs and snoring dog, and her mother insisting that she was just like the princess who could feel a pea under twenty mattresses and twenty feather beds. Lil, who flicked off her headlamp and settled in on the floor across from Penny, just listened, the candlelight casting lovely shadows on her face.

When Penny finally ran out of steam, Lil said, "I think you're giving peas a bad rap."

Penny was indignant. Was that all Lil had gotten from what she'd said? "I don't see what that's got to do with…"

Lil raised a hand to shush Penny. "Could I take you somewhere tomorrow? If you're free, that is. I want to show you
something. And then, if you still want to eat your gross peas,
well, fine, eat your gross peas. But I really think you should see
it before you go on with this."

Penny peered into the pot. The peas looked even more
revolting now that she'd scooped into them. And tomorrow
was her day off. "Um. Okay. I guess."

"I have to work in the morning, but I could swing by at
about one."

Penny tucked a blonde curl behind her ear. Should she be
making this kind of commitment when she was high on champagne? "Sure," she said, not at all sure that she was.

Lil stood. "Good. I'm going to turn the breakers back on."

A yawn slipped from Penny's mouth. She tried to disguise
it with a smile. There was no way she wanted Lil to think the
yawn had to do with their date. Or was it a date? Her brain was
so muddled from the champagne she really had no idea. But she
knew she had to say something. "You fixed it?"

"Won't know until the breaker's back on, but I found some
loose wires. If this doesn't work, I'll come back tomorrow to
check the switch. You want me to turn off this switch so you're
not blasted by light when they come back on?"

Another yawn threatened to slip out, but Penny held this
one back. "That would be nice."

Once Lil was out of the room, Penny stretched out on the
couch next to a purring Screech. His soft rumble made her
eyelids heavy. She let them close. Once again, she felt comforted
by the sounds of Lil in the bedroom. She moved with such confidence, such self-assurance.

Penny pulled the throw blanket from the back of the couch
and tucked it in around herself and Screech. What was she

doing making a date with someone she'd just met? Again she wondered if it actually was a date. Maybe Lil just felt sorry for her. That seemed more likely. Who'd want to make a date with a sloshed crybaby obsessed by peas?

She woke briefly when Lil blew out her candle and slipped out of the apartment, clicking the door shut softly behind her. At some point in the night, Penny made her way to her bedroom where she slept uninterrupted until noon.

She awoke feeling refreshed, excited and a bit nervous about her date.

Once out of bed, she checked the light. Sure enough, the flicker was gone. She padded her way to the kitchen where Screech rubbed up against her leg as if she might forget to feed him. "Okay. Okay. Hold your horses." As she reached for the cat food, she noticed a note on her counter weighted down by the pot of peas.

Miss Penny,
*   If you've changed your mind about today, call me.*
*   335-3700. Otherwise I'll see you at 1:00.*
*   Lil*

She smiled. No one had ever called her Miss Penny before.

As a reminder not to get her hopes up, she dumped the loose peas into the garbage disposal then filled the pot with water to soak the rest of them out. *You barely know her.*

At one sharp there was a knock at the door. Penny glanced in the mirror. She'd been unsure how to dress so had chosen casual: jeans, her favorite tank top that showed just a strip of midriff, and sandals. She was glad for her choice when she opened the door. Lil was wearing shorts, a T-shirt and work boots.

"You still up for this?" Lil asked.

Penny picked up her purse. "If you promise it'll keep me from eating those gross peas."

Lil laughed. "I can't promise, but I have a hunch."

As they walked down the stairwell, Penny couldn't help but feel sheepish about the night before. "Thanks for fixing my light."

"No need to thank me," Lil said. "It's my job. Besides, it was my pleasure." She unlocked the passenger side of an old pickup. "And this is my chariot."

Penny slipped in. The interior was meticulously kept up and smelled as if it had recently been wiped down with something slightly citrus. "Nice," she said when Lil came around the other side.

"Thanks. She might not be fancy, but she's paid for." With that, Lil turned the key in the ignition and pulled into the light Saturday stream of traffic.

A wave of panic passed through Penny. She barely knew this woman, and now here she was in a truck with her going to god-knew-where. She tried to think of something to say. "So, what was wrong with the light?" was all she could come up with.

"The usual. A few of the wires were loose. It can happen over time."

"Especially when you have a guy upstairs who jumps rope."

"In his apartment?"

"Monday through Friday. Six a.m. Right above my bed."

"You shouldn't have to put up with that."

"What choice do I have? He pays his rent just like I do."

As Lil seemed to be mulling this over, Penny sat back trying to appear casual and observed her driving.

She moved through traffic with confidence, like she belonged on the road. And she stopped for pedestrians. This was something Penny appreciated, as she herself did not have a car so she was often walking. And yet there was something about Lil's confidence that also frightened Penny. Where was she taking her?

Just as she was about to ask, Lil said, "I'm going to talk to Mr. Baratelli."

"The landlord?"

"Yup. He and I have a pretty good rapport. I'll let him know that the reason your lighting fixture needed work was because of unnecessary physical activity upstairs."

"You don't have to do that."

"I want to. I hate the thought—" Lil slammed on the brakes to keep from hitting a blue Mazda that had run a stop sign. Her arm instinctively reached across to protect Penny. "You okay?"

Shaken, Penny said, "Fine."

When Lil removed her arm, an unexpected longing passed through Penny. "My dad used to do that," she said.

"He didn't want anything to happen to his precious cargo."

"I don't know about precious."

Lil glanced at her briefly before returning her attention to the sudden cluster of traffic. "I do."

Penny looked out the window and said, "Thank you," very softly. Who was this Lil? And why was Penny still apprehensive?

A few minutes later they pulled up to a row of Victorians that had been split up into apartments. "Mine's the blue and gray one," Lil said. "I'd invite you in, but one of my roommates is down with the flu. No need exposing you to that."

Penny cocked an eyebrow. "So why did we come here?"

Lil smiled. "You'll see. Now follow me." And before Penny

knew it, Lil was out of the truck and making her way down a small dark walkway between two Victorians.

Penny hopped out of the truck and trotted behind. What was this girl up to?

The walkway opened up onto a large community garden.

Lil stepped to the side of the entrance made of marvelously twisted wood, bent slightly at the waist and swept her arm wide. "After you."

Penny, acting all serious, pretended to lift a heavy ankle-length skirt, tilted her chin toward the sky and stepped through the arbor, then stopped dead in her tracks. The garden was stunning. Rows of raised beds, each scrupulously kept up, filled the quarter-acre plot. And there were little sculpted sitting areas here and there—and wind chimes.

Penny walked over to a bed lined with luscious green. "Is this butter lettuce?"

"The best in the world." Lil grinned. "And completely organic." She broke off an outside leaf. "Want a taste?"

Penny opened her mouth and Lil tucked the crisp leaf between her lips. The back of her hand gently brushed the side of Penny's cheek.

Was that on purpose? Penny wondered. A slight shiver passed down her spine as, with great care, she closed her mouth around the lettuce leaf. It would be the freshest thing she had ever eaten and she wanted to savor it.

"Oh, my god. It's so…"

"Buttery?"

"It is! Store-bought never tastes like that."

"Taste this," Lil said, ripping off a dark green leaf from another plant.

An impossibly sweet burst exploded in Penny's mouth. "What is that?"

"Italian parsley."

"Parsley? I thought parsley was just something you got on the side of your plate at a restaurant."

Lil popped a sprig into her own mouth. "I use it for a breath freshener." Then she walked over to a raised bed full of beets and carrots. "Soon we'll be putting in the summer stuff. You know, tomatoes, squash, eggplant."

"Who's 'we'?" Penny asked, suddenly praying it wasn't a girlfriend.

"Our collective. But I'm one of the main ones. I work out here almost every day."

Penny watched as Lil tenderly inspected the underside of a broccoli leaf. "I had no idea broccoli grew like that," she admitted.

"Isn't it beautiful? The heads are actually flowers."

The thought of eating flowers delighted Penny. She brought her nose to the broccoli head and inhaled. It didn't smell like a flower but had a rich musky scent. "Yum."

"I'll make you up a bag of produce before you go." Lil took Penny's hand. "But now let me show you why I brought you here."

Penny let herself be led to the back of the garden, loving the feel of her hand in Lil's. They fit so perfectly, Lil's larger, stronger hand wrapping around her smaller, softer one. "Thank you for blowing out my candle last night."

Lil gave her hand a squeeze. "Seemed like you were having a pretty rough night."

They rounded a tall trellis covered in climbing green vines.

"Voila!" Lil said. "My pride and joy."

Penny laughed. The vines were covered in pea pods. Of course! She stepped in for a closer look and noticed thread-like tendrils reaching out from the vines to curl around to the slender bamboo rods of the trellis. Along with the pea pods, each vine was sprinkled with the most delicate white flowers. Apparently peas started out their lives as flowers.

"Now these are birthday peas," Lil said. "Go ahead. Pick as many as you want."

Penny glanced at Lil, her grip on Lil's hand involuntarily tightening. "You expect me to eat these?"

"Why not? You were going to eat those crappy burned ones last night."

"But they're not cooked."

"Don't tell me you've never had fresh peas off the vine."

Embarrassed, Penny shook her head. Until last night, she generally avoided peas altogether.

Lil let go of her hand and plucked a pod off the vine. "Promise to keep an open mind?"

Penny nodded. What choice did she have? This woman, who she was finding herself more and more attracted to, was offering up what she called her "pride and joy."

Lil slid her finger down the seam of the slender pod and cracked it open, revealing six perfectly round peas. "Take one," she said as she stepped in close enough for Penny to smell her clean, parsley-scented breath.

Much as Penny was excited by the sudden intimacy and Lil's obvious delight in the peas, she couldn't help noticing a mild nausea heating up her belly. *What am I doing? I hate peas.* But she couldn't refuse, not after all the trouble Lil had gone to. So she braced herself for yet another disappointment, and said, "Okay. I'll try."

She chose the plumpest one, right in the center, and tugged lightly. The round orb popped out easily. Now she'd have to eat it. Or at least put it in her mouth. Lil's hopeful gaze was giving her no choice. She slipped the pea between her lips. The small

hard ball rested on her tongue, so innocent, so devoid of expec-
tation. She rolled it around in her mouth a couple of times,
testing, then without another thought bit down.

"You like?" Lil asked.

Penny thought for a moment and, to her surprise, found she
wasn't the least bit repulsed. It was sweet. Fresh. Nothing like
the bland peas of her childhood. She took the whole pod from
Lil and, using her tongue, flicked the rest of the peas into her
mouth.

Lil laughed. "I guess the answer is yes."

Penny wanted to say the answer was more than yes and that
this was the best birthday present she'd ever received—in her
whole life—even if it was a day late. But before she could put
this thought to words, Lil pulled another pod from the vine,
popped it open and let the peas tumble into her palm; only this
time instead of offering them up for eating she just let them rest
there. "It just blows my mind that inside each of these peas is
the beginning of a whole plant."

"Kind of like people," Penny said softly. "Each one of us is
full of so many things that nobody knows about. Like you with
this garden."

Lil picked up a pea and pressed it to Penny's lips. "I'd like to
know more about you. If you'd let me."

Penny let her lips curl around Lil's fingertip and linger for a
moment, then took the pea into her mouth and circled it with
her tongue before biting down and swallowing. "I should tell
you, I'm not always easy. I can be kind of like…"

"A princess. You told me. But from what I've seen, you're
the real thing."

An icy wall inside Penny began to melt, releasing a single
tear. She brushed it back.

Lil let the peas in her hand drop into the rich soil and rested both hands on Penny's shoulders. "What's more, I think real princesses deserve to live happily ever after."

The warmth of Lil's hands made Penny's knees go weak. "I'd kind of given up on that whole notion."

Lil cocked her head. "You'd given up on peas, too. So what do you say we give this princess thing one more try?"

I THINK I WILL
LOVE YOU

Rebecca S. Buck

The rising moon was a milky haze in the blue satin sky. The faintest sprinkle of stars held the promise of the beauty to come, when twilight deepened into night and the rich indigo faded to inky black. The breeze of a midsummer dusk crept over my skin, still sticky and heated from the day, soothing and chilling in the same breath. The woodland in the valley below rippled softly, a sound like a gentle flow of water, as the wind crept through the leaves of the tall oaks and chestnuts that predominated there.

The scents of a summer evening in the central European countryside reached me, carried in the cooling air. The heady fragrance of flowers, honeysuckle with a trace of petunia, the nostalgia-laden essence of freshly cut grass and the slightest acrid tinge of wood smoke from a smoldering fire somewhere on one of the farms farther down the valley. The day had been overpoweringly, swelteringly hot, and the earthy odor of sun-baked soil beginning to grow damp as the atmosphere cooled made it impossible to forget I was anywhere other than the middle of the countryside.

No artificial lights illumed the streets here. Someone across the valley had turned on an electric lamp in their house, and the bright square of the window etched a vivid point of yellow against the black shadows of the hillside. Everything was shadows and silhouettes now, not quite obscured by the night, not yet, but otherworldly and mysterious already. The dark green of the trees, the depths between them, made a patch of almost total blackness in the valley bottom. Above that, the hillside seemed to recede into the farther distance, darker stripes marking out where the terraces of grapevines grew, row after row. Paler, more regular shapes demonstrated where cottages dotted the hillside opposite and the hillside beyond it.

The almost oppressive silence was the one part of country living I had yet to become accustomed to. It wasn't a true silence—a faint breeze rustled in the trees, an animal scuffled in the undergrowth. I even heard the distant throb of a tractor engine, but compared to the English city I had lived in until almost a year ago, this was a muted, whispering world, and though I admitted it was peaceful, I found it also left me unsettled from time to time. I could only fall asleep if I had the radio murmuring quietly in the background. Silence left too much space for thoughts to creep in, and I had, after all, moved to another country to distract myself from thinking too much. Isolation I could deal with; I enjoyed it and found plenty of things to do to fill my time. But I had to have noise. Silence combined with isolation was just pushing this escape too far.

I reclined the sun-lounger I was relaxing in until I was more lying than sitting and let my eyes drift out of focus, staring blindly at the darkening skies. I was relaxed. I was at peace. If I wasn't truly happy, what did that matter? There was no one here to see it, no one to subject me to merciless sympathizing, endless cheering up and interminable relationship advice. I could cope with unhappiness. It wasn't as though I was a stranger to it, after all. And I'd really known from that first week that the thing with Kimberly was never going to work. I'd just clung to her out of some sort of unbalanced need to demonstrate that I was attractive, my skills of seduction had not yet dried up, and I was capable of turning a night of passion into something longer and more meaningful, even if I wasn't head over heels in love. Of course it had all ended when I discovered that she had been clinging to me in a similar capacity, with the added complication of an ex-girlfriend she was still in love with and desperately trying to prove that she was not.

Life was simpler here, in my little cottage in rural eastern Slovenia, surrounded by trees and grapevines, and neighbors whose language was largely incomprehensible to me. Much simpler. I sighed and closed my eyes because that wasn't true anymore, not as of a month ago. A month ago, everything had grown far more complicated again.

Karmen Jurkovič. On a hot day in May, my closest neighbors had invited me to a birthday party in their garden. Self-conscious and out of place, the invisible wall of language difference making me at once the subject of curiosity and too awkward a prospect to attempt a conversation with, I was contenting myself with glasses of the local sweetly floral Traminec white wine and enjoying the early summer sunshine. Then I had seen her walking toward me, petite and dark haired, with smooth olive skin and sharp, almost black, eyes.

"*Dober dan,*" she had greeted me tentatively, though her stance demonstrated plenty of self-confidence, which she had every right to. Close up she was beautiful, in a striking sense. Not pretty, perhaps even a little sharp featured, but indisput-

ably beautiful. Blue jeans clung tightly to slender thighs and
a perfectly formed waist, and a red halter-neck top revealed
toned, slightly angular shoulders with pronounced collar-
bones beneath that smooth, dark skin. Her hair was cropped
short, and unlike that of most of the women in this part of the
world, still its natural glossy black, not dyed or highlighted red
or blonde.

"*Dober dan,*" I had replied, keen to demonstrate I could at
least manage a greeting in Slovene.

"*Kako si kaj?*" she enquired, asking how I was.

"*Dobro, hvala, in ti?*" I managed, telling her I was good,
thanking her and returning the enquiry. My accent received the
sympathetic smile it deserved.

"*Dobro tudi, hvala,*" she returned, with laughter in her tone.
"You are English girl?"

"Yes, I am." I offered her my hand, and she took it, "Carolyn,"
I told her. The hand that gripped mine in return was strong-
fingered and warm.

"Karmen," she informed me. "I am student of English, but I
am very poor."

Deciding that it wouldn't be polite to begin correcting
awkward phrases when we had only just met, I simply smiled.
"Do you live near here?"

It turned out she was from the nearest town, called Ljutomer,
about ten minutes by car from my cottage. We'd talked for about
half an hour before we'd been called over to take part in the
lighting of candles on the mass of cream and sponge that passed
for a birthday cake. Before she left, she had given me her mobile
phone number, and we'd decided to meet for coffee in town in
the next week. She told me talking to me was good practice for
her English, and that I could maybe learn some Slovene from
her. I worked hard to convince myself that was the only reason

I agreed to meet her again, swallowing the attraction I felt. She was stunning. Of course I felt attracted. There was no need to act on that feeling every time I felt it. Besides, the chances of her returning the feelings were slim to none. I wasn't aware that I'd met another lesbian since I'd been here. I wasn't sure where they were all hiding in this country, but it certainly didn't seem to be in the hills, vineyards and villages of brightly painted houses that surrounded my home. Honestly, I preferred it that way. The quaint conservatism of the people here asked no questions, so I told no lies. It made things simple at least. The likelihood of one of the most attractive women I'd met here being gay was so slight that it wasn't even worth contemplating.

So when we'd met for coffee and Karmen, after some pointed questions about my lack of boyfriend and the exchange of a smile in which there seemed to be an unspoken acknowledgment of the connection between us, began clearly flirting with me, I'd been surprised, but happily so. It was pleasant to play the game with her, amusing to listen to her attempts at flirting in English, which were far more fluent than anything I could have attempted in Slovene. I'd felt the warmth growing inside me as we'd talked, and an unexpected feeling had come. *I could love you.* The sudden intensity of it had made me draw in a sharp breath. I wasn't in love with her yet, but I could sense it hidden not far away in my emotions, ready to bubble to the surface. Forcing myself to relax once more, I'd enjoyed the notion, happy that I wasn't emotionally dead after all.

It was later, alone in the silence, that I had grown frightened. I could have misread the situation. One thing I had learned here was that, even only a few countries away from home, the conventions of body language and manners were considerably different from what I was used to, and Karmen's phrasing was not always straightforward enough to follow. And even if I had understood her intentions clearly, which I suspected, not being entirely an idiot, I had—that was even more frightening. I'd sworn that I wouldn't get myself involved with anyone else for at least a full twelve months.

Three relationships in three and a half years had ended in disaster. The fault had been partly mine in the last two, but in the first I still considered myself blameless. They'd all hurt, a white-hot burning that shocked my heart, and I still could not grow immune to that sort of pain. Hence my self-imposed exile in the northernmost part of the former Yugoslavia, a little-known corner of Europe sandwiched between Austria and Croatia, Hungary and Italy, where it seemed likely I could hide from all my problems. Meeting Karmen had made it uncomfortably and frighteningly apparent that I could not hide from myself. I'd sent her a text two days ago, when we had been due to meet for coffee once more, and told her I couldn't make it. It would be safer not to see her.

Now, I let the ever-deepening darkness envelop me and tried not to think about her, or my dismal relationship history. Maybe I was just meant to be alone. I certainly never felt lonely in my own company.

The sound of a car approaching along the road from town penetrated the night. Moments later headlights appeared over the crest of the hill, yellow and bright in the deep twilight, as the car descended toward my house. I waited for the familiar swoosh of air as it passed but instead I heard the engine slowing and the unmistakable crunch of tires on the gravel driveway at the front of the house. My heart thudded. I hated being caught off guard by visitors. I wondered if I could stay hidden. There were no lights in the house, no evidence that I was home. If I just stayed silent here at the back of the house maybe whoever it was would just go away?

I heard the sound of someone knocking on the front door. About thirty seconds later whoever it was knocked again. Then there was nothing, and I felt relieved that he'd given up so easily. But in the next moment I heard the whisper of footsteps in the grassy lawn to the side of the house, and, *"Dober večer?"* Good evening.

The Slovene accent is not dissimilar to the Russian, but with the dual twists of a more Mediterranean musical tone and a harsher Germanic pronunciation. In Karmen's deep voice, even the simple greeting sounded wonderful. My heart fluttered. Why was she here?

"Karmen?" I demanded, sitting up in the lounger, as she appeared in the shadows at the corner of the house.

"You are hiding?" she asked, matter-of-factly.

"No, just sitting in the garden."

"Oh, I see. It is quiet here."

"Yes."

"I come to see you. I want to give you this. Cookies!" She handed me a foil packet. I unfolded the wrapping to find several slices of what smelled like chocolate and rum cake.

"Thank you. But this is cake, not cookies," I corrected, because she'd told me to whenever she made a mistake.

"Ah, yes, cookies are different, I remember. And you, in England, you call them...what is it?"

"Biscuits," I supplied.

"Ah, yes. I made the cakes by home."

"You mean they're homemade? Well, *Hvala lepa,*" I expressed my gratitude, touched by the gesture since Karmen didn't really seem like the baking type.

"You are welcome. I—*kak si reče?* Looked for you?"

"Er...you mean...er?" I replied, trying to follow her train of thought.

"When you sent me message, I wanted to see you," she insisted forcefully.

"Oh, you missed me?" I clarified, glad of the gloom since my face flushed as I said the words.

"Yes, that's right. I missed you," she agreed, and I immediately wished it was light enough to see her expression.

"Thank you." My heart was surging again. It was no good. I needed to see her face, that voice in the darkness was too much for me. "Do you have your lighter?"

"What?"

"Er, your, er...fire, for cigarettes?" I knew Karmen, like virtually every other woman I'd met here, was an occasional smoker—with coffee, after a stressful day—and always carried her lighter.

"Aha, yes." She fished about in her pocket for a moment and produced the lighter. I took it and reached over to the surface of the upturned log I used as a small and uneven table out here on the patio behind the house, where I lit the citronella-scented candle that stood in a terra-cotta dish. The flame flickered and then flared into brightness bathing us in a halo of amber light. I looked up at Karmen as she stood by the side of my lounger. Her face was half in light and half in shadow now, magnifying the dark of her eyes, the sharpness of her features, even as she smiled. That smile was enough to make me glad she had come to see me.

"I'm sorry you missed me," I told her. "I was just too busy that day." I didn't really want to lie to her, but I couldn't admit to my cowardice either.

"What were you doing?" she pressed, and I got the distinct sense that she saw right into me. The breeze made the candle gutter, shadows playing wildly over her skin as she looked back at me with those intense eyes. She almost made me lose all of my self-possession.

"Oh, you know..." I shrugged and looked away from her.

"No, I do not know," she replied, with characteristic bluntness. Tact wasn't a common Slovene trait and she had none whatsoever. Maybe that was what I needed. "I think you were afraid."

"What of?" I challenged, though I didn't deny her conclusion.

"How can I know?" She raised her hands in a small gesture.

"Of you?" I wondered if that was what she thought. She was very intense after all.

"I hope not, I am not to be afraid of. Maybe you afraid of you?" There was enough light for me to see the way she raised her eyebrows in question, though her tone suggested she knew she was right. I stared back at her, dumbfounded for a moment. However much had been lost in translation between us, her understanding and perception of me were clearly sharp and accurate. "I do not understand however," she went on when I didn't reply. "One day you will become death, and then you will know that life was too quickly."

"You mean life's too short?" I said quietly, though I'd understood her well enough.

"Yes, that is what I mean." She sounded mildly irritated by my correction this time.

I could say nothing in reply, and she was silent too. The night was thick and increasingly black now, the moon still hazed by light clouds that obscured many of the stars. The brightest light was the candle flame reflected in her feline eyes as we contemplated each other. Despite the cool of the breeze, I felt hot suddenly, claustrophobic in the silence, and longed for some noise to break the tension between us.

I jumped when she took a step toward me. When she tried to take the foil-wrapped cake out of my hands, I almost hung on to it, as if it protected me somehow. She tugged it free and placed it on the log next to the candle. The next moment her legs were astride the lounger, as she faced me and lowered herself into my lap. She was very petite and light, and the lounger didn't even groan as it took her extra weight. Which is more than can be said for me. It was all I could do to repress the sound that threatened to escape my lips. The contact of her thighs against mine, and now her hands on my shoulders, sent a bolt of heat through my entire being. My head felt light and a heaviness settled between my thighs.

"You want me?" she asked.

"You seem to know that already." I tried to laugh, not succeeding through the thickness in my throat. My heart beat wildly as she moved her face a little closer to mine. She smelled of body heat, floral soap and a hint of cherry-sweetness.

"I want you," she said simply, and the accented words were more eloquent than anything she could have said had she been a native English speaker. Her face came closer to mine, and before I could even think about it, our mouths were melting together. Her lips were hot and soft, but surprisingly insistent. Her kiss was a tease at first, and I allowed my lips and tongue to dance with hers in return. It was when, with a moan into my mouth, her tongue pushed in harder, with more apparent lascivious intention, that I felt the surge of fear rising inside me, overriding the heat she stirred in my blood. I pulled back.

"It's not a good idea," I told her. I was doomed to failed relationships, and I didn't want Karmen to be another one of my victims. It always started this way—from the flirting to the irresistible kiss, to the ripping off of clothes and the first night of the best sex ever. It was usually the morning after that I found things started to deteriorate. Either I wasn't emotionally mature enough or it was just cruel destiny. I didn't want a relationship

with Karmen that I'd remember for great sex and then a gathering sense of impending disaster. Still the thought came; *I could
love her, some day soon.* If we went too far now, the chance of
that was gone.

She was still sitting astride my thighs, her body warm where
it crushed into mine. That ache low in my abdomen cried for
attention, but the warnings of my heart, my sudden awareness
of what it yearned for, were stronger. Karmen was looking at me
curiously, and I was relieved she wasn't offended.

"But what is wrong?" she inquired, a new softness in her
tone.

"I can't. I mean, I want to, but I don't..." I tried to explain
incoherently.

She leaned in again and brushed my lips with hers, oh, so
lightly. My whole body stirred. "Carolyn, I don't want to fuck
with you."

Not sure quite how she meant her statement, I was silent for
a moment, waiting breathlessly to see how she would continue.
"For me you are very beautiful. I want to look at you and to kiss
you and talk with you. I want only to go to bed with you if I
love you. I do not love you now." She said it so plainly, with her
soft tone smoothing the edge of her accent, that her words were
hypnotic to me. I couldn't imagine a girl in England saying the
same things to me. Not the girls I'd met anyway.

"I don't love you either. Yet," I told her in a whisper, leaning
forward to kiss her tentatively and with a little more passion
when she returned the pressure. The spark of arousal reignited
inside me, but I allowed the fire to spread through me, relishing
it, knowing I didn't have to act upon it. I wanted to kiss her and
look at her too.

"You know, it does not have to be so fast," she murmured,
"we can go slow." She kissed me again, deeper but slowly, sensu-

ally. My body came alive for her, but the overwhelming urge was to wrap my arms about her slight form, just feel her close to me. It was such an innocent need, compared to my usual lusts, and its novelty made it intoxicatingly wonderful to me.

"I think I will love you," I breathed, pulling back from her for a moment and reaching up to stroke her smooth face. She trailed a finger from the corner of my moistened lips, over my throat and between my breasts, over my T-shirt.

"I think maybe I will love you too. And then it will be hot between us," she replied, and in the promise, the anticipation, I found a greater arousal than anything I'd ever known, since that first, nerve-fueled time all those years ago.

She pressed toward me once more, her hands reaching for mine. My hot fingers entwined with hers as our lips met and parted, as our tongues caressed and explored gently. She moved into me, and I felt the swell of her breasts against my own, the warmth of her body close to mine. Stunned, I realized I needed nothing more but that tender mouth, the reassuring grip of her fingers, our shared heat and the promise of a love that could grow. We'd planted the seed and watched the first green shoot push to the surface. The blossoming fulfillment would take patience and cultivation, but it could—and would—come.

The evening had become night. The heady floral fragrances of twilight faded with the lingering remnants of the day. The night was emptier than the dusk, colder, but Karmen filled my senses now. An owl hooted in the woods, and the trees rustled their flowing music in the breeze, but my surroundings were like a dream. I was only aware of Karmen's breathing, the throb of her heart in time with mine, and the echo of those accented words, *I think maybe I will love you too.* Tonight, in the flickering candlelight, they carried magic with them, and I was transported out of the dysfunctional life I had grown accustomed to, the constraining fear that had descended upon me, and swept into the realm of possibilities.

CAMELLIAS

Anna Meadows

S hore Vista in late July and early August—the most well-
manicured ghost town on the face of the earth. BMWs and
Land Rovers are tucked into garages. Mail has been put on hold.
Children clad in J. Crew or Lilly Pulitzer don't run on the side-
walks, because they've either been shipped off to Grandmother's
house, or taken to Santorini or Nice with their parents.

Everything else runs as though the residents were still here.
Walkway lights stay on their timers. Landscapers, paid in
advance, still come to trim the hedges and see to the begonia
borders—because you never know when *Architectural Digest*
might be stopping by to snap a few photographs.

The sprinklers still soak the sod lawns to keep them green
as malachite. If they didn't, the grass would turn to straw in the
heat, the same heat that drives families from the area on yearly
vacations scheduled to coincidence with the area's two or three
scorching weeks.

Shore Vista residents pay yearly dues that include guard-

attended gates, private security and a homeowner's associa-
tion that decides what three colors the houses can be painted
each year. Only a few residents, my cousin and her husband
included, hire house sitters: some because they have a collection
of rare orchids whose gravel needs humidifying on an hourly
basis; others because they've just remodeled and want someone
looking after their granite countertops and smooth-coated walls.
In my cousin's case, she has two cats and can't bear to put them
in a kennel, which is where I come in. I can count on everything I bring to my cousin's house being covered in orange and
calico fur by the time I leave. Saffron and Cinnamon curl on my
clothes, nap in my suitcase and sleep on my head.

Most summers house-sitting is a way to pick up extra money.
This summer it's how I'm scraping by. I lost my job last month
when the dress boutique where I worked folded, and a rent hike
forced me out of the apartment I had leased for a year. Half my
stuff is at my parents' house, the other half is with friends.

I've been doing this just enough summers to know by muscle
memory that the kitchen and living room are upstairs, not
down, and the bedrooms are downstairs, not up. After I turn
off the alarm, I tuck my bags into the guest room, water the
hanging fuchsias and make sure nothing's on that's not supposed
to be. Then I get my clothes off as quickly as I can, stripping
off my jeans and cooling my bare feet on the guest bathroom's
travertine. My inner thighs are clammy, my hairline damp with
perspiration.

The Henleys next door are out of town until the end of the
month. They left my cousin the gate key so I could use their
pool, and I want the sun-veined water against my skin so badly
it's like my body is thirsty.

I dig through my bag for my two-piece. When I don't find it
in the main compartment, I search the outside pocket, then the

laundry pouch and the side zippers. I empty my clothes and hair dryer and toothbrush onto the duvet. But when it's all spread out on the bed and floor, my swimsuit isn't there. It's in a box at Jenna's apartment or in my mother's craft room.

I don't feel right looking through my cousin's drawers for a suit I can borrow. For all I know, she only owns one, and she's taken it with her to sun on a private veranda with her husband. I throw on my clothes and grab my wallet, because the drugstore in town sells cheap suits as bright as traffic signs.

The far end of the street, pitch-black with new asphalt, ripples like boiling water. My car's seats hold heat from the windshield in their dark vinyl, and the metal of the belt buckles is so hot I can barely get them fastened. If I drive to the drugstore, I'll melt in the driver's seat by the time I park. Saffron and Cinnamon will starve. My cousin's fuchsias will wither to potpourri. Burglars will use stethoscopes to break into the safe for the jewelry, snatching my cousin's twelve-speed blender, her husband's basalt mortar and the good sheets on their way out.

I go back inside and take my clothes off again. Holding a towel around my body, I check to make sure the walls around the Henleys' backyard are tall enough to block the view from the cul-de-sac, the palm fronds thick enough to hide me from other house sitters in upstairs windows or terraces.

The gate falls shut behind me, and I let the towel drop to the sandstone deck. With a dive from the deep end, my hands pierce the still pool, then my arms and shoulders. The water swallows my bare breasts and hips, and my body finishes its arc as my ankles and toes vanish under the surface. The cold tingles across my skin, and light bows through the dark pool like slow lightning. I hold my legs together and kick, and my hair cuts through the blue like dark kelp. Circling my arms, I arch my back and turn over, reaching for the blueberry-colored bottom and then for the light.

When I open my eyes, I see a blurred figure standing in the yard, back to the pool. Startled, I fall from my orbit and breathe in. I cough to clear the water from my nose and throat, flailing to get above water.

I break the surface and throw my head back to clear my hair from my eyes. Now's she's in the pool, waist deep, the legs of her overalls full with water, and her hair half-covering her eyes. One of her overall straps is unhooked, leaving one side of the bib hanging away from her body and revealing the curve of her breast, the only way I'm sure she's a woman.

She doesn't come closer, and I scramble to climb onto the deck and wrap the towel around me.

"I didn't see anything." She lowers her head more and backs up toward the steps.

I'm about to dart for the gate and toward the house to call the police when I notice the dirt-stained gloves on her hands. A canvas sack, sagging with clippings, leans to one side near the rosebushes, hedge trimmers sitting at its base. A crate of nursery pansies sits in the shadow of a camellia bush in bloom. I dove into the pool so quickly, I didn't notice if they were there before.

"You're the gardener," I say.

She nods once, pulling her soaked pants from the water. They drag on the deck, darkening the stone.

I hold the towel tighter under my arms. "You trying to swim with your clothes on?"

She hooks the undone buckle on her overalls. "Looked like you were drowning."

I smooth the towel behind me. "I'm not trespassing. Or crazy."

"I know. Henleys said you'd swim." She wrings out her pant hems. "But I figured it'd be with something on."

The bottoms of my feet are drying, and I shift my weight on the hot stone from one to the other. I look down at the terry cloth, barely spanning my breast to my thighs. "I forgot to pack my suit."

She inclines her head, but doesn't look up. "Didn't mean to scare you."

I keep my left forearm against my chest to keep the towel in place. Leaving seems rude. I wonder what kind of small talk I'll need before it won't.

I hold out my hand. I expect the scent of pool water clinging to my skin, but I smell like a sea tide. I always forget the Henleys use salt, not chlorine. "My cousin lives next door. Her and her husband."

She pulls the glove from her right hand and shakes mine. "I do their yard too. Few others on the block."

I walk on the balls of my feet toward the gate. "It's beautiful."

She puts her glove back on. "Don't not swim. 'Cause of me."

"I'll buy a suit."

"I'd lend you one, but I don't swim."

"Don't want to mess up your hair?"

She laughs and ruffles her grown-out pixie. "Sure."

My hair soaks the back of the towel, and I gather the strands onto one shoulder. "I'm sorry. I should've waited. Until I bought one."

"Nobody else here." She kneels next to the pansies. "I don't care." She kneels in the grass and plunges her hands into the soil. I slip out the gate, trying to close it quietly behind me, but the latch clatters as it shuts. I run back to the house without looking to see if she's turned her head to watch me go.

* * *

The last of the sun dissolves into the ocean. The sky turns bright as sherbet before it deepens to turquoise. But the heat doesn't go with the light. It thickens in the house, warming the area rugs and bobbing up against the ceiling like a hundred helium balloons. Even the night winds don't disperse it. They only ruffle tree branches and flower bushes, pushing the air through the leaves like a hair dryer on low.

Cinnamon scampers to the kitchen as soon as she hears me rattling food into her bowl. Saffron stays curled on an uphol-stered chair, blinking slowly to tell me she'll eat her dinner when she's good and ready.

I drop an ice cube on the kitchen floor for Cinnamon, my cousin's way of getting her some exercise. The cat bats it near the fridge and the cupboard, chasing after it when it skids toward the living room, almost frictionless against the tile floor.

Saffron follows Cinnamon with her eyes without turning her head. I go after Cinnamon to make sure she doesn't abandon the ice cube where it will soak a sofa dust ruffle as it melts.

Cinnamon follows it out to the balcony, where overhanging palm fronds shade the tile from the day's heat. The ceramic feels warm under my bare feet, but not hot. Breezes part the branches, and the lit blue of the Henleys' pool flashes into view. The warm wind pulls whole camellias from their bushes, and their petaled rounds spot the grass with pink. A few land in the pool, and the blush-colored flowers turn slowly on the surface of the dark water.

I went into town earlier to pick up groceries and ice, but I didn't buy a suit. I couldn't bring myself to wear a bikini the color of a crossing guard's vest, or a one-piece as fluorescent as a yield sign. They're the discount version of the kind of clothes everyone in Shore Vista wears. Men play golf clad in pants as pink as indigestion tablets. Women favor dresses that match the tennis balls at their private lessons. Children run through sprinklers in vitamin-orange shorts and frocks as bright as blue neon. It's like they're all trying to be seen from space.

The gardener will be gone by now, but I throw on a bra and panties in case the Henleys have their housekeeper stopping by. I step through the grass, careful not to crush the fallen flowers. I don't dive in because I don't want to disturb the ones floating. A splash might fill their shallow cups, causing them to sink, and I want them to stay, patterning the blue. My fingers graze the polished rail, and I step in slowly, one step at a time, first to my ankles, then my calves, my hips, my waist.

One of the garden lights at the far end of the yard seems to flicker, and I see the gardener's shadowed figure kneeling by the far flower bushes. I stumble off the last step and grab at the water like it will help me get my balance, but my palm only slaps through the surface.

She turns her head at the noise.

I climb the steps to get out. "Sorry."

She stands up and comes into the light. "You don't have to leave."

I slowly sink back down the steps. "You work nights or something?"

"I'm staying till they're back." That one overall strap is undone again. When she catches me looking, she fastens it. "Looking after the place."

I stir the water, sending the flower heads spinning. "They never hire a house sitter."

"Daughter got a beta. Threw a fit when they didn't let her take it, so they promised her they'd get someone to look after it."

"They're paying you to feed a fish?"

"They wanted me to pull out the viola beds and replant

anyway, so I'm around." She kneels on the side of the pool and dips a garden glove to the water to fish a camellia head from the surface.

My hand flies to hers before I think about it. "Don't."

She looks up.

"They're pretty." I bend my head and hide behind my hair, embarrassed at touching a stranger. "When they wither I'll get them out."

She blinks instead of nodding, and I let go of her hand.

I swim under the camellias, darting near their shadows on the bottom of the pool. Between their spinning petals I can see her working in the flowerbeds, her outline softened by water.

I surface and feel the noon heat drying the fine strands along my hairline. "Come in," I say.

She barely turns her head toward her shoulder.

"Come in." I cross my arms and prop my elbows on the warm sandstone on the side of the pool. "You'll melt in those clothes."

"I'll be all right."

"I'm decent today. I promise." I hold the rail and climb the steps until she can see my bra and panties. Water runs from the lace down my back and thighs, and I check to make sure the fabric hasn't gone translucent, hinting at the brown tips of my breasts or the dark triangle of hair between my legs. But the nylon is only a shade or two lighter than the pool. Nothing shows. "See?"

"I'm not much of a swimmer," she says.

"Don't know how?"

"I know how."

I climb out and cross the grass toward her, blades sticking to my wet feet. "Nothing to be embarrassed about." I crouch in the grass next to her flat of nursery pansies. "If you don't."

"I know how to swim."

My fingers graze the heavy denim of her overalls. "You'll die in these."

She shudders, her irises barely visible through the hair in her face, and my hand opens and freezes on the side of her thigh. The shiver spreads through her back, her shoulder blades and muscle showing through her thin shirt. Her fingers gently tighten and loosen on the packed-dirt pansy in her garden gloves. I kiss her, and she drops it, the outside layer of soil shaking free from the flower's stem.

She falls back into the grass, and her palms spread the cold of damp earth down my spine. I kneel on her, straddling her hips and weighting her down in the grass. The right side of her overall bib is loose, again. I take the undone strap in my hands, laughing.

She props herself up, her elbows behind her. Her bangs shadow a shy smile. "What?"

I twirl the strap on my fingers. "You've always got one loose."

She shakes the blush from her face.

"It's always the same one," I say.

"It's cooler. Lets air in."

"If you're hot, why aren't you swimming?"

"Don't want to."

I reach to undo the left strap.

She stiffens.

"What?" I ask.

She shakes her head, wriggling out from under me.

I slide off her. "What's the matter?"

She leaves her gardening gloves in the grass and goes toward the house.

* * *

I swim the next afternoon, and I don't see her. I stay until evening and don't see her. I look out for her until the end of the week, and she stays gone.

Each night I fall asleep to the soft clicking of Cinnamon chasing an ice cube down the hallway, and I catch myself gripping a handful of sheet and remembering the soft weight of her breast in my palm, covered in thin cotton.

The flat of pansies stays untouched in the grass. Early in the morning, they catch the spray of the lawn sprinklers, and the violet petals don't wither. Each evening the night winds pull more camellias from the bushes, so that the lawn is half-covered in them. They carpet the surface of the pool in red and white and blush pink. By the time they're so thick that not even a slice of salt water shows through, I'm sure I imagined her, the messy hair, the earth-stained fingers of her gardening gloves, the half-fastened overalls.

Cinnamon bats the last of her ice cube against the hallway wall. She slides it away and strikes it so it ricochets against the molding again. I groan from half-asleep to awake and flick on the light. Saffron sits in the middle of the floor, blinking at me like I should stop Cinnamon from making such a racket, since I gave her the ice in the first place.

Shifting the ice cube from one palm to the other, I get Cinnamon to follow me upstairs. I throw the balcony doors open, taking the ice and tossing it onto the warm deck. Cinnamon chases after it, and I lean against the railing and watch to make sure she doesn't slip through the bars down into the yard. Slouching, I rest my elbows on the sculpted brass and wait for the next breeze. But just as it comes, Cinnamon sends the ice cube skidding back into the living room. I'm about to go back inside when the palm fronds part enough for me to see into the Henleys' yard.

The gardener stands by the pool, hands in the pockets of her overalls, watching the stirring of pink and red petals. One side of the bib is undone, like always. My shoulder blades pinch when I remember cupping her breast. I press my lips shut to keep from gasping when she reaches for the other strap and unhooks the buckle. The other side of the bib falls away from her chest, the strap and buckle falling down her back. I turn off the porch light, hiding behind the thicker palm branches. The heat lies so heavy on my body it feels like it's covering me, keeping me invisible.

Pulling the socks from her feet, she steps into the pool. The solid cover of flowers ripples away, revealing a ring of glowing blue around her ankles, then her legs, her thighs and waist. She undoes the side buttons on her water-darkened overalls and steps out of the legs. They drift away from her body, floating among the camellias before sinking. She leaves the last step, and her briefs disappear under the blossoms. Water and petals lap at the hem of her undershirt.

The wind rattles my cover of palm fronds, and she glances up and sees me. I jump back, but she doesn't startle, keeping my gaze. She knows I've been watching her, and I know I can't run inside like I want to.

She parts her lips. A deep inhale lifts her shoulders. They fall again when she breathes out. I take the rubber band from my hair and let the strands fall to my shoulders, trapping the heat against my upper back. Still watching me, she pulls off her shirt, reaching behind her and tugging it off by the back of the collar. She holds her arms over her chest before I can see her breasts.

She's still there, her arms still hiding her, when I get to the backyard. She doesn't move, and I stay back near the gate.

"Fell off a horse." She tosses her head, clearing her bangs

from her face. "I was thirteen. Didn't get checked out for a couple years."

I come closer with every word she says, but I can't help shaking my head, because I don't understand.

She holds her left arm tighter against her. "They said my mammary artery was so shot this side'd never come in right."

My eyes settle on her upper body. Her left breast holds her right arm from pressing flat against her, but her right forearm is straight against her chest.

Coming toward her so slowly my bare feet are silent against the sandstone, I follow her into the water, dispersing loose petals.

"I knew her. That horse." She fidgets with her own body, digging her fingernails into her sides just above her ribs. "I shoulda known she was in one of her moods. Shoulda known she wanted to throw someone."

I stand in front of her, sliding my hands under hers and pulling her arms away from her chest. She tenses, but I hold her hands to my hips and she lets her shoulders go slack. I cup her breasts in my hands and kiss them, my lips grazing the full left one, then lingering on the smaller right one that barely curves from her chest.

She closes her eyes and unhooks my bra with two fingers. It falls to the water and floats with the flowers. She pulls my panties down to my knees. I step out of them and let them sink to the bottom.

I come closer so she doesn't have to reach for me. My slight movement shifts the current, floating her hand toward my body. I part my legs to let her find me. Her fingers graze my folds and she shudders, letting her other hand fall to the hollow at the small of my back.

"Sorry." She tucks a damp camellia into my hair. "For running."

I slide my mouth onto hers and reach for her briefs. She bucks a little as I move the waistband down her thighs, to help me get them off her or because she can't help it. We pull each other into the water, letting the blooms hide our bodies. She keeps one hand on my back, the other between my legs, and I grab the insides of her thighs to hold on to her. Her briefs and my bra drift with the camellias, the only evidence we were ever there, until we surface again.

THE PANACEA

Colette Moody

Their flirtation had started months ago, essentially on a dare. Hope had noticed the leggy redhead within the first week that she started working at the downtown coffee shop and had committed her name to memory the instant that Hope first scrawled it on the side of the paper coffee cup—Simone. The name seemed perfect for her. It was sexy, alluring and classy.

While it wasn't unusual for Hope to remember the drink orders of the regular customers, she took special pride in remembering Simone's brew of choice. Of course, the fact that Simone came in every morning on her way to her upscale office job didn't hurt matters. Hope was always impressed by Simone's business attire—frequently silky in nature, sometimes low cut, other times slit high and always provocative yet tasteful.

It had been a coworker, Tim—the shift supervisor no less—who had dared her to do it. He insisted after Hope had been working there only a month, that he was tired of listening to Hope "blather on" about Simone—her sultry voice, radioactive smile, warm eyes and what Hope had deemed "an ass so magical that David Copperfield might climb out of it at any moment."

"Christ, Hope," Tim whined as he dumped the house blend into a coffeemaker and prepared for the shop to open. "Why don't you do everyone a favor and just hit on her already?"

"Because, boss," she hissed as she busily stacked cups, "I'm not supposed to come on to the customers. Besides, what if she's straight? And not just regular-straight, but like…crazy, circus-freak straight?"

Tim scowled. "What the hell is 'circus-freak straight'?"

"You know, where people pay money to slip into a tent and stare at the woman who despises lesbians. As fodder for the crowds, they occasionally show her a picture of a boob and she curses them to hell before she vomits."

"You think if she knows that you have the hots for her and her magical ass, that might taint her chai latte?" he asked, chuckling.

Hope sighed. "She doesn't drink chai. Besides, I'll settle for just hearing her raspy voice call me 'babe'…just once."

"Seriously?" Tim was standing and blinking at her incredulously.

"Dude, have you not *looked* at her? If she purred something like that at me, I might just come in my pants."

His expression changed and became mischievous. "Well, that's an easy enough theory to test."

"What do you mean?" Hope asked suspiciously.

He disappeared for a moment into the back room, before reappearing with a basic, thirty-dollar label maker. He typed something on its tiny keyboard, tore off the gray strip that emerged from the side, and peeled off its adhesive backing. Tim smirked as he stuck the label on Hope's name tag, effectively obscuring her name. It now read BABE.

"You're an ass, Tim."

When Hope reached to remove the label, Tim lightly slapped her hand away. "Ah-ah-ah. She'll be in sometime this morning, right?"

"Right."

"So let's see if we can make your dream come true," he said. "If nothing else, it's a hell of an icebreaker, right?"

"Not to mention a great way to get a free slap," Hope added.

Tim appeared smug. "Look, I'll give you complete permission to hit on this chick. In fact, I'll put money on it."

Hope's left eyebrow rose. "What kind of money?"

"Twenty bucks says you won't openly flirt with this girl."

She considered this for a moment. "You're on, brother."

"And I'll double down if you flash her a tit."

As she had every morning the preceding four weeks, Simone entered the coffee shop between 7:35 and 7:45—right in the middle of the morning rush. When Hope spied her in line, she gave Tim the agreed-upon signal—she began to sing Dionne Warwick's hit "Do You Know the Way to San Jose?" at the top of her lungs.

He jerked his head around from the espresso machine, squinted at the line and grabbed Hope by the waist. "Let's switch."

Hope nodded and went off to start making the coffee orders, leaving the cash register to Tim.

Had she not been cranking out the cappuccinos as fast as her fingers could manage, Hope would have found the time to wonder exactly how she was going to flirt with Simone. Instead, before she knew it, she held an empty paper cup with the name SIMONE written on it.

She took a deep breath and began crafting the half-caf caramel wonder that she knew would touch Simone's lips. She made sure the foam was perfect, then turned, flashing the most charming smile she could muster. "Simone, your coffee is ready," she murmured breathily.

Simone looked as beautiful as she ever had, her auburn hair cascading over her shoulders and her navy-blue business suit hugging her plentiful curves in all the right places. She returned Hope's smile as she advanced to the counter, ready to pick up her frothy beverage, and the sight of her approach caused some kind of cranial misfire in Hope's cerebrum.

"Uh…"

Hope suddenly recalled that she was obligated to flirt with this woman. They had, after all, put money on it. She looked to Tim who was somehow watching her while he took people's orders at the same time. She glanced down and realized that she had yet to hand over the java, and Simone just stood across from her, waiting for it to be offered.

"I'm sorry," Hope finally said. "You're just so beautiful, I completely forgot what I was doing."

Hope was waiting for her horrible prophecy to be fulfilled, but Simone did not recoil. She didn't even appear to be thrown off kilter by the comment. Instead, she studied Hope for a long moment, before she reached out and took the cup. "Thanks very much." Simone's eyes dropped to Hope's name tag. "Babe."

Had Hope wanted to conceal her delight, she was neither emotionally or physically equipped at that moment to do so. Her grin reached no doubt from ear to ear.

"Is that your real name?" Simone asked, as Hope felt her pulse begin to race.

"No, but it sure was nice hearing you say it."

Simone seemed more than simply flattered as she tasted the

coffee, never once breaking eye contact with Hope. "Mmm. Well, I can't wait to see what your name will be tomorrow."

"Have a great day, Simone."

"You too, Babe."

Hope watched Simone saunter out the door and head down the sidewalk, before Hope once again regained her wits. She suddenly noticed the other customers who were waiting for their drinks—now all staring at her as though she had just pulled down her pants and smacked her ass for them. "Oh," she said self-consciously.

A haughty patron crinkled his nose and crossed his arms defensively. "You think you can get it back in your pants long enough to make my soy latte, honey?"

"Sorry," Hope replied, her elongation of the first consonant emitting an awkward whistle.

Tim leaned in and whispered in Hope's ear. "I'll give you the twenty, though I'm disappointed there was no tit."

"Well, there's always tomorrow."

Since that day, every morning Monday through Friday (barring any federal holidays, of course) Simone came into the coffee shop, placed her standard order and made it a point to have some exchange with Hope—sometimes brief, but always saucy. Hope found it frustrating that Simone never came in at a time when they weren't absolutely slammed, though part of her thought it might have been intentional.

Certainly the notion of a straight woman flirting with a lesbian was not a new one for Hope. And that situation might be made even safer when the lesbian only had about forty seconds to speak before a hostile caffeine addict shouted at her to hurry up and get her "ass in gear."

The seductive parlaying between them went back and forth

for seven months, and while Hope was sane enough to recognize that she had irrationally developed a fascination with Simone—a very strong crush perhaps—their playful flirting made her feel so good that she just went with it, trying to push the boundary infinitesimally with each passing encounter.

One misty spring morning, the rush of customers was slower than most days.

"Here you go," Hope said, holding the cup out so that Simone had to take it from her, causing their fingers to brush incidentally. "Can I assume you're wearing that low-cut blouse for my benefit?"

Simone smiled seductively as she took the coffee. "Of course. And are you wearing anything for my benefit?"

"You can't tell from that side of the counter, but I'm not wearing pants."

Hope found Simone's laughter almost musical. "Well, that leaves me a lot to think about over the course of my workday."

"Good. Why should I be the only one horribly distracted all day?" Hope asked before leaning in toward Simone and crooking her index finger to draw her closer. "I put some shaved chocolate on the top for you. Don't tell anyone," she whispered.

"You spoil me."

"I'd like to," Hope replied softly.

A tiny bit of foam had drizzled down the side the cup, which Simone seductively licked before sucking the remnants off the tip of her finger. "Well, chocolate is a very good start...and so very versatile."

Hope swallowed loudly. "Did I already mention that I find you immensely distracting?"

Simone's smile was terrifically naughty. "Now that you mention it, I believe you did. See you later, Hope."

Hope watched her sashay out the door—her vision riveted to

Simone's tight tweed pencil skirt.

"Good god almighty," she exhaled reverently.

As Hope wiped down the inside of the coffee shop windows later that afternoon, she was surprised to see Simone shuffling down the sidewalk in her direction, holding an open cardboard box full of office supplies. She was visibly upset, and Hope had a sudden sinking feeling.

"Hey, Simone," Hope called, holding the door open. "C'mere."

Simone stopped and seemed to ponder the request.

"C'mon in," Hope insisted. "I'll buy you a drink."

As Simone walked into the coffee shop, her sassy confidence from earlier that morning was gone, replaced by a dispirited dejection.

"Something tells me you're not having a good day," Hope said, taking the box out of Simone's arms and setting it on a table in the corner window. "Layoff?"

Simone sniffed. "They're calling it a 'strategic workforce reduction.'"

"Wow, and what are you calling it?"

"Anal rape," Simone replied bitterly.

Hope winced. "Ouch! I'm sorry, honey. Look, have a seat here. I'll be right back." She slipped behind the counter and whipped up a frozen concoction in a blender before pouring it into two small cups and returning to join Simone at the table. "Try this. It's my own creation."

Simone stared at the cup and sighed. "You know, I saw it coming...for months, but I was trying to stay hopeful. I thought I was just being paranoid. I'm such an idiot."

"Completely untrue. So how many got cut?"

"Eleven of us." Simone tasted the frozen drink and her expression softened slightly. "This is really good. What is this?"

"Something I mix up for myself when I need a little boost. I call it the panacea. It brightens the spirit, clears the mind and cures both consumption and dropsy."

"It's so velvety and thick. What's in it that makes it so good?" Simone asked, taking another big sip.

"Ah, that's either the opium or the unicorn tears." When Simone glanced up at Hope briefly with only subtle amusement in her eyes, Hope decided to try another tack. "Are you okay?"

"I don't know. I think I might be in shock."

"Are you getting any severance?" Hope asked, crossing her legs and studying Simone's face.

"Four weeks worth."

Hope cleared her throat awkwardly. "So, do you have some astoundingly lucky significant other waiting for you at home who can take up the financial slack while you look for another job?"

"If that's your way of asking me if I have a girlfriend, no. I'm single."

Hope was slightly heartened by Simone's use of the word "girlfriend," but out of sympathy tried not to look gleeful. "What about a roommate? Friends? Family?"

"I moved to the city for this job, so the only friends I've made in the nine months that I've lived here are the ones at the office who just watched me pack my shit into this box and get walked out of the building." She combed her fingers nervously through her hair.

Simone's plight was breaking Hope's heart. In the months that they had been friendly, she had never gleaned a tenth of this personal information. "So what are you going to do now?"

"I have no fucking clue. I suppose I could start drinking heavily." Simone looked at her watch. "If I get started now I could be vomiting before dinner."

"It's good to have goals, I suppose," Hope said weakly. "You just need to take a little time to collect yourself and then get right back out there into the job market...which I know sounds totally shitty."

"Only because it is shitty, Hope. Maybe this is the city telling me to quit while I'm behind. I've been here the better part of a year, and I don't have anything to show for it—not a goddamn thing."

"Or, at the risk of sounding like a cheerleader on ecstasy, I'd say you could view this as just a temporary setback—one of life's curveballs. It's not like you're unemployable. It's the economy, not you. You can bounce back from this."

Simone was inconsolable. "I should just head home and start packing—just start accepting that I'm a failure."

"Hmm, I have a better idea. How about instead of pulling out that dog-eared copy of *The Bell Jar* so you can scrawl suicidal notes in the margins, you go out with me tonight?"

"I don't know," Simone said softly. "I can't imagine being good company right now."

"Hang on, before you totally reject me, hear me out. I understand that you're clearly not in a very social mood, but this really is more about you not having to go home and lie on your sofa in the fetal position while you suck melted Häagen-Dazs through a straw."

"But I'll be a total drag," Simone countered, slurping up more of her drink.

"And I get that. I'm not asking you out so you can entertain me. There's no pressure at all. I'll treat you to a happy, fluffy movie."

Simone shook her head adamantly. "No way. I'm not having you pay my way for anything. I'll be a financial burden to the state soon enough. I don't need to branch out and be a burden to other people too."

Hope was duly chastised. "Fair enough. I won't spend a dime on you, okay? You can just come over to my place and I'll make you dinner. We can just hang out."

Simone did not seem sold on the idea. "I don't know."

"So *The Bell Jar* and the Häagen-Dazs still sound better than time with me? Have I mentioned that I cook for a living?"

Simone looked around the empty coffee shop. "I thought this was what you did for a living."

"This is my day job," Hope explained. "Four nights a week I'm a line cook at Le Chevalier."

"Wow. That's impressive. And somehow I apparently don't even do one thing well."

Hope picked up the paper towel she had been using to wipe down the windows and tossed it on the floor. "Sorry, there's a flag on the play—illegal self-pity."

Simone smiled. "What's the penalty?"

"Loss of down, and you have to let me help you feel better. Come on, Simone. Why not try to salvage the rest of what's started out to be such a shitty day?"

"Okay," Simone relented.

Hope was unable to hide her elation. "Do you live near here?"

Simone nodded.

"Well, luckily for you I just live a couple blocks away. So here." Hope scrawled her address on a clean paper towel and pushed it across the table to her. "Come on over anytime after four. We can eat around seven, if that's okay."

"You forgot your phone number," Simone said, sliding it back over to Hope.

"I wasn't born yesterday. If you have my number, there's a chance that at ten of seven I'll get a call from you saying that you've changed your mind. Then I'm stuck with six gallons of uneaten Beanie Weenie."

"Um…"

"In my defense, my Beanie Weenie kicks ass," Hope said with a grin. "Do you have any dietary concerns I need to know about? Sugar? Gluten? Red meat?"

"I do it all."

Hope blinked. "You know, when I imagined you saying that to me it was a completely different scenario, but somehow I still found that exceptionally hot."

A flash of the flirty Simone emerged, and she winked before finishing off her drink and setting the empty cup on the table. "Okay then, I'll see you tonight." She took Hope's address and dropped it into her cardboard box. "Should I bring anything?"

"Do you drink wine?"

"Yes."

"Then you're in charge of the wine. Bring whatever you like."

"Okay," Simone said, standing and throwing away her trash. "Thanks, Hope," she added softly as she backed into the door and slipped back out into the street.

Hope thought that she had never met anyone more adorable.

Simone couldn't believe she was doing this. Twenty-four hours ago she had been gainfully employed and her life had been structured and certain. Now she was jobless and on her way to a date with someone who, with her bad luck, was perhaps a lunatic barista.

She climbed the flight of stairs in Hope's apartment building, clutching the paper bag that shrouded her wine bottle, as though it were a cudgel. With every few steps she vacillated between acknowledging that she found Hope very attractive, coupled with her thankfulness to have a social diversion to keep her mind off losing her job, and the unsettling fear that she really didn't know this woman at all. What if she had sixty-three cats? Or an ex who arrived in the middle of their meal, angrily wielding a cleaver in one hand and a dildo in the other?

Simone sighed. This was why she had been single for so long. After a couple of twisted, contentious relationships in the small town she used to call home, she now tended to buy into every lesbian stereotype there ever was and thereby talked herself right back into a life of eating alone and involuntary celibacy.

She thought again about why she was so drawn to Hope. She always seemed to be in an upbeat mood, and as corny as that seemed, Simone really liked that—it made facing her mornings in corporate purgatory more bearable. She also appreciated the style Hope possessed. She clearly had an affinity for bold colors and silver jewelry, and many times Simone had admiringly watched Hope's strong, capable-looking hands as she made coffee or counted back change. Hope was witty, smart and sexy—that's just all there was to it.

She arrived at Hope's door and knocked rapidly, before she could talk herself out of it. When the door opened, Simone was unprepared for the sight of Hope in her nonbarista attire. She was wearing a simple white blouse over a sexy silk camisole, and faded low-rise jeans that didn't just accentuate Hope's hips, but sang her body electric.

"Wow," Simone said spontaneously. "You look...great."

Hope smiled, glanced down at her outfit and shrugged. "You just haven't seen me without a paper hat and cappuccino foam stuck in my hair. Come on in."

Simone felt instantly sheepish. "Thanks." Suddenly remembering that she had wine, she offered it. "Oh, and here's the wine."

Hope pulled the bottle from the bag and examined the label.

"Mmm, this will be perfect."

"Great," Simone said, trying to focus on not saying anything else stupid. "What are you cooking?"

"Well, I'm trying out a new dish tonight," Hope said, taking the merlot and beginning to uncork it. "And you're going to be my guinea pig. If you like it, I'll propose it to the head chef, and we'll see what he thinks about adding it to our menu."

"Well, it smells delicious."

"Thanks. That's Gorgonzola Beef Wellington, and I'm making you my famous shallot and bacon polenta…in case the Wellington sucks." Hope filled a wineglass and handed it to Simone.

"I'm sure it won't suck." Simone scanned the roomy studio apartment. It was clear that the kitchen was the focal point, but though the furnishings were simple, there was an easy, artsy feel to the place. She noted the bed in the corner. There was no other. "Your apartment is great. You live here alone?"

Hope took a sip of her newly poured merlot and seemed pleased with it. "Yeah, it's just me, Eleanor and Bettie."

Simone bit her lower lip as she looked around. Three women could not sleep comfortably in one queen size-bed—fuck like mad women perhaps, but not sleep. "Are they here?"

"They're always here," Hope replied, pointing to a bowl on a bookcase with two goldfish in it. "They're homebodies. Girls, this is Simone. Simone, this is Eleanor Roosevelt and Bettie Page."

"That's a peculiar combination."

Hope chuckled. "Well, at the risk of sounding crazy, I've always had this idea that if Eleanor Roosevelt and Bettie Page had met, and…perhaps been roommates, it would have made for a hilarious sitcom. One is an intellectual civil rights advocate, and the other is a kinky fetish queen with a righteous rack—but which is which?"

Simone found that image so funny, that she laughed until she snorted, most indelicately.

"So come on outside, and I'll show you where we'll be dining." Hope took Simone's glass, set it down and led her by the hand out onto the fire escape, where she plugged in an extension cord and strings of cobalt patio lights turned on. There, Hope had set up a small table, linen napkins, fancy china and a vase of freshly cut irises, while below in the distance were the sounds of traffic and the city.

Simone covered her mouth as she took it all in and suddenly became emotional—as though everything that had happened not just that day, but since she had moved to the city, was finally brimming to the surface. "This is beautiful," she said softly. "You didn't have to go to all this trouble."

Hope looked unusually serious. "It's no trouble. I just wanted there to be something about today that you could feel good about."

Any reservations that Simone had been harboring were instantly gone, and she stepped forward and kissed Hope deeply.

When they separated, Hope looked pleasantly surprised. "Was that an 'I find you irresistible' kiss, or more of a 'you're sweet in a nonsexual way' kiss?"

Instead of replying, Simone took Hope's face in her hands and tried again, this time in a way that could never be described as "nonsexual." As Simone's tongue moved provocatively, she found Hope's mouth tasted sweetly of red wine. Hope kissed her back and Hope's hands came to rest tenderly around Simone's waist as the kiss ended.

"Did that answer your question?" Simone rasped.

The corners of Hope's mouth rose slightly and she shook her head. "Unfortunately, I'm pretty dense. You may have to show me a few more times before I start to understand."

Simone looked into Hope's smoldering blue eyes. "I think that can be arranged."

Hope's lips slid seductively along Simone's exposed neck and collarbone as her hands moved to the small of Simone's back. "And when you're done, I've got a few things to show you...if you're interested."

Simone had not felt desire like this in quite some time, though it was perhaps exacerbated by her already hyperemotional state. She brought her mouth close to Hope's ear. "I'm interested," she said softly. "Another panacea perhaps?"

Hope was deeply affected by the quickening of Simone's breathing. "We can certainly call it that, if you like. Though it may require extensive and repeated doses."

Simone pulled back slightly to search Hope's face, and the want and gentleness that she saw soothed her wounded soul. "This treatment, is it habit-forming?"

"God, I hope so."

"I think I hope so too."

Hope's eyebrow arched. "So maybe you should hold off on packing, huh?"

Simone bit the inside of her cheek. "Well, at least until I've tasted the Wellington."

"I had no idea the Wellington would be a deal breaker," Hope laughed.

"Well," Simone breathed, in between kisses, "if you can cook and kiss this well, I don't stand a chance."

"Mmm, good."

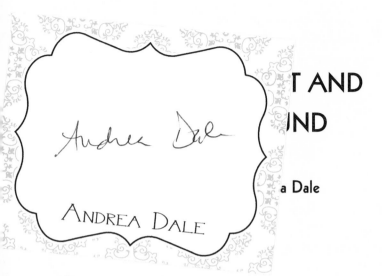

Andrea Dale

ANDREA DALE

An all-expenses-paid trip to Hawaii? Sign me up!

So what if I got slammed with a massive last-minute freelance accounting job from a well-paying but notoriously flaky client the day before we left? But, hey—have laptop, will travel. I could make my deadline if I hunkered down in the hotel room.

Except for when I snuck out to take surfing lessons from some sloe-eyed, sultry native pro...

I went from that lovely fantasy on the plane to standing forlornly in the baggage claim area, watching the empty carousel go round and round.

The airline folks wrung their hands. *So sorry,* they said. *Really feel bad about this,* they insisted. *We'll do everything in our power to find the suitcase,* they promised, *but there's only one flight to this island per day,* they apologized, *so it may take time....*

"Oh, my god, Lara, I'm so sorry!" Jeanne's eyes were wide with compassion. She hated traveling—which was why she'd asked me to tag along while she gave a workshop at the annual Women's Proactive Retreat and Conference—and this was a personal nightmare of hers, ranking right up there with being thrown in a Thai prison for accidentally smuggling drugs.

"I'll be okay," I said, putting on my gamest smile. "I've got a change of underwear and a toothbrush in my carry-on, at least. That'll get me through."

I could handle this. I squared my shoulders. I've backpacked around Europe for six months, I've boated down the Grand Canyon for sixteen days with only what I could carry. I could make do until they found my luggage.

I'd pick up a few essentials at a discount store—they did have Target here, right? Or at least Walmart?—and get by.

Or so I thought.

No, the smaller islands didn't have discount stores (what was I thinking?). And we were bussed right out to the resort, where my only option was the gift shop—in which the cheapest T-shirt was more than I'd be willing to spend on a new dress.

Let's not talk about how much the dresses cost.

Not to mention the bathing suits. There was a gorgeous shimmery copper one, sturdy enough for laps in the pool but pretty enough to catch the eye, but it was far, far out of my budget.

The next morning I poked at my travel shirt, which I'd handwashed the night before. Still damp.

About the only positive thing I could grasp on to right now was the fact that the hotel rooms had nice plush complimentary robes. I ordered the cheapest thing I could get by on from room service, wincing at the cost, but I couldn't go wandering down to the dining room in the robe, you know? Hopefully Jeanne would swing by before lunch and have time to grab something for me.

The accounting books, as usual, had not only been late, but

were a mess. I scowled. I couldn't even escape from them for a swim or a walk to ogle sloe-eyed, sultry natives....

There was a knock at the door. Couldn't housekeeping see the bloody DO NOT DISTURB sign? As tempting as it was, I was too polite to shout, "Go away!" so I opened the door.

Well, hello. Apparently my despair had been a call, because a sloe-eyed, sultry native had come to me.

She wore adorable little black rectangle glasses and a cool white wraparound top that showed just a hint of cleavage, as well as a Women's Conference badge.

My heart leapt. "They've found my luggage?" I leaned out to peer behind her.

"No, I'm sorry," she said. "I'm Evie, with the conference. Your partner told me about your missing suitcase."

"Jeanne's not my partner," I said, because suddenly that was a much more important fact to clarify than the whereabouts of any silly suitcase. "We're just good friends."

"Oh!" said the delectable Evie. "Oh. I'm sorry."

I laughed. "Really, not a problem. What can I do for you?"

I tried not to think too hard about what I really wanted to do for her. Or to her. Damn, but I didn't normally fall in lust so…instantaneously.

But she had the cutest dimple, and I just wanted to lick it, for starters.

"I wanted to help you out," she said. "If you'll give me your sizes, I'll ask around and see if any of the other attendees have clothes you could borrow. Or maybe take up a collection so you could buy a few things." She leaned in conspiratorially; I smelled a fruity sort of perfume or maybe sunscreen. "The prices in the gift shop are just *insane*."

Thank god it wasn't just me.

I backed up to let her in. "I'd feel really weird if people paid for my clothes," I said. "I'm not even attending the conference."

She collapsed onto the bed, her skirt riding up to show a yummy expanse of tanned, toned leg. "I see your point," she said, "but I think it would actually make them feel good. Helping a sista, don't'cha know."

I laughed. "True. But I really don't need a new wardrobe; I just need a few things to get me by until my luggage arrives."

"I like you," Evie said, flashing that damn dimple again. "You have a highly developed sense of optimism."

"If I didn't laugh, I'd have to cry," I said. "Why doesn't this island have a Kmart?"

"Hm," Evie said. "There *is* a lone dollar-store-type place two towns over. It's pretty cheesy, but it might do the trick."

She'd be able to steal a couple of hours after lunch, and so I worked like a fiend to get as much number-crunching done as I could before then.

That was hard, because my mind kept wandering back to Evie and that dimple and the way she'd said, "I like you," and even though I had no idea if she liked girls, I was imagining her straddling me, saying, "I like you," as she dipped down for a kiss, or pinned beneath me, saying, "I like you," as I feasted on her pert nipples. (Score one for the air-conditioning in my hotel room, which had left me pretty certain she hadn't been wearing a bra.)

That lack of bra continued to work to my advantage, because journeying two towns away involved driving over some bumpy dirt roads. I watched out of the corner of my eye while keeping up my end of the conversation.

I was thrilled when, in answer to my question, "What do you do for fun?" she said she surfed.

"That's something I've always wanted to try," I said. "I've

water-skied…is it very different?"

"There's more balance needed, but if you have the basic skills, it's not that hard," she said. She flashed that dimple again. "If you're free Sunday afternoon and the conditions are good, I'd be happy to show you the ropes."

Oh, I'd be free, all right. I'd stay up all Saturday night working if I had to.

Then we got to the dollar store, and all bets were off again. They didn't have any bathing suits.

I came away with a couple of Hawaiian-print sarong-type skirts and some basic T-shirts in matching colors, which would get me through the rest of my stay. The only beachwear they had were a couple of eensy bikinis, and I'd have had to sew at least three of the bra cups together to cover one of my generous womanly gifts.

I grabbed an extra T-shirt, a hot-pink touristy thing that proclaimed ALOHA! in exuberant, swirly, aqua print. Maybe I could get away with it and a pair of panties for a midnight dip in the ocean when nobody else was around.

On the way back, we stopped at what looked like a ramshackle shack teetering precariously on a cliff, but in fact was a restaurant serving the best fish tacos on the planet. I swear I wanted to be alone with mine.

But I *was* alone with it—and with Evie—and that was even better.

As she gazed out over the view that I admitted was spectacular, though not as spectacular as she was, I wondered again whether she liked girls.

It was now or never. I refused to run from a challenge. "Thank you," I said, and then I leaned over and brushed a kiss across her cheek, inhaling that sweet sunscreen scent.

If she didn't get it, so be it.

She got it. As I drew away, she turned her head. Our lips were inches apart.

"Oh," she said, curving her mouth in a naughty, dimpled grin. "Do that like you mean it."

Could anyone refuse an invitation like that? I brushed my fingers along her jaw, urging her closer, watching her until her eyes fluttered shut and our lips met. Then I couldn't keep my eyes open, either.

She tasted like salsa, hot and spicy. Our tongues met, flirted, succumbed to the age-old dance.

On the table, our fingers twined. A slow, warm glow started in my belly, spreading lower as if I were bathed in sunlight from the inside. My nipples tightened and my groin followed suit, pressure building.

Just from that kiss.

Finally, reluctantly, she pulled away. "Wow," she said. "I hope that was as amazing for you as it was for me."

All I could do was nod.

"I wish I could sit here and kiss you for hours," she went on, "but I'm afraid I've got to get back...." Her hand squeezed mine. "Can I see you tonight?"

Again, nodding was my only available option. She'd left me speechless with delight.

I realized, as I tried to focus on work and failed miserably, that I was nervous. Why, I wasn't entirely sure. She was cute, she was interested in me; what was the problem?

The problem was that I really *liked* her. I'd never been into flings per se, but there had been times when the planets aligned and I'd had a juicy time with a like-minded girl, no strings attached.

Evie lived in Hawaii (on Oahu, granted), and I was from

Chicago. What kind of future could we have?

And why was I thinking about the future anyway?

After the dry air-conditioning in the hotel, the sultry night air was a relief, soft and sweet smelling against my skin. I was to meet Evie in one of the cabanas, far down the beach. The closer cabanas were filled with women who'd spilled out after the conference activities officially ended at ten; I found Evie in a more secluded one, with its own little cove.

She'd laid out leftover hors d'oeuvres from the conference, along with a bottle of wine and a multitude of candles.

I was hungry—to keep the cost down I'd been getting most of my meals out of the vending machines—but at the same time, I didn't want to eat too much. I nibbled juicy chunks of pineapple and mango, tasted spicy shrimp skewers and let sweet wine and conversation flow.

Finally, though, before I could talk myself out of it, I leaned in and kissed her again.

Her skin was salty and sun warmed even now, this late, and I was shaking right down to my dollar-store panties, a heady combination of nerves and lust.

The nerves mostly faded as the kiss progressed, thanks to her enthusiasm. It's hard to have self-doubts when someone's kissing you with so much fervor that you nearly fall off your chair.

When we broke apart, we were both breathless.

"I have something for you," she said.

"I bet you do," I murmured.

She laughed. "That's not what I mean—not right now, anyway. Here."

She held up a resort-logoed bag. Inside, I found the shimmery copper bathing suit from the hotel gift shop.

"Some of the women heard about your luggage and had

already started pooling their money," she said before I could protest. "Anyway, it's for tomorrow. For when I give you your surfing lesson." In the candlelight, I saw the wicked glint in her eye. "Tonight, though, you won't be needing it. Up for a swim?"

If I'd been thinking more clearly, I would've understood that she was suggesting skinny-dipping—which I had no problem with any time—but when she pulled her top over her head, my tongue stuck to the roof of my mouth.

Her tanned skin gleamed in the candle flames, and from the lack of lines, I knew she didn't wear a suit very often even in the daylight.

Stop staring and strip. Stop ogling her teardrop breasts and thinking about how you want to take those fat nipples into your mouth.

I compromised and multitasked: I stripped while fantasizing and catching glances as often as I could.

The water was so calm, so utterly smooth and pristine that I felt a pang of reluctance at disturbing it. But Evie grabbed my hand and urged, "Come on," and then we were running out together, laughing as the sand shifted beneath our feet and the drag of the water slowed us down.

We dove and swam and bobbed in the amazingly warm, buoyant water, and when we paused to catch our breaths, I licked her dimple and kissed her again.

She was saltier and wetter, but her tongue was warm as we got more serious. I was through playing, done with questioning myself—now I wanted her, and I wanted her now.

I pressed against her. She was taller than me, but the ocean's effect on my breasts meant they were pretty much in line with hers. I moaned into her mouth when I felt my nipples press against her and hers against me.

Bliss.

Beneath the soft water, she slid her hands over my hips, into my waist and up between us, gently urging me back so she could cup my breasts. She rolled my nipples between her fingers, gently at first and then harder as I hissed, "Yes. *Yes,*" and the sweet electric shocks of pleasure rippled through me.

I sank my teeth into her lower lip, not hard, just tugging and sucking. It wasn't enough, so I backed toward shallower waters, just enough so her torso was exposed and I could feast on her the way she had touched me. Her mews of delight made my head swim. I could've nipped and licked forever, just to hear her gasp and beg for more.

More was what we both wanted, almost to the point of frenzy. I molded my hands to her pert ass, slid lower. The water was warm, but her core was molten like the volcanoes that had formed this island. I wanted her to explode like those volcanoes.

One, two, three fingers slid inside her sleek, tight wetness, while my thumb ground against her hard clit. With another woman, in another place, I would have wanted to lay her out, lick and tease and explore, but with Evie, right here and right now, I wanted to feel her come.

I wanted to make her come.

When she did, pulsing and undulating around my fingers, I swallowed her screams in a kiss. My own clit shivered in empathy, not quite an orgasm but with the same rhythmic throbbing as Evie's climax.

She fumbled down and stroked me, and I shuddered and rocked against her fingers, pressing my face against her collarbone and begging for mercy.

She gasped about not having a roommate, which was all I really needed to hear. (Jeanne was a dear friend, but I wanted time alone with Evie: wanted, desired, needed, required, would murder for.)

Tomorrow we'd surf. Tomorrow, maybe we'd talk about the future, if there was any sort of future to talk about.

Tonight, though, was about being lost in the tropics with Evie.

A WITCHY WOMAN CALLED MY NAME

Merina Canyon

Lacey wanted everyone to call her Lance, but she had a hard time getting us to do it. I liked to call her *Lace,* which was what her mama called her before she died. Lacey told me she hated to be called Lace because it sounded like the worst part of being female—being enslaved in the kitchens and sewing rooms. I had to laugh at that 'cause I spend a lot of time tending the home fires myself. "No Lace for you then, Sir Lancelot," I said from behind my checkout stand at the grocery store. "Ain't no skin off my teeth."

Lance loves her cowboy clothes and boots and always has her curly black hair cut short like a boy. My hair is short too, but not *that* short. She has these icy blue eyes with long eyelashes and a constant just-woke-up look. She'd come into the store every day for her Red Bull and Snickers, and some folks accidentally called her sir till they looked her straight on and saw her mother's Spanish beauty looking out. She didn't actually want to be a man—she just wanted to be treated equal with a man, with the same sort of respect for her dare-devil strength out on the ranch where she works.

She probably would have gone on just trying to prove her equal strength to men and wandering aimlessly through life if it hadn't been for that witchy woman, Gwen.

The one time Gwen came into the store is branded in my memory. She was some kind of sandal-wearing, stunning woman with long brown hair tenting down her bare shoulders. She had on a white summer dress and just seemed to have magic sparking off her. I'd say she was about my age—thirty-three, about six or seven years older than Lance.

Gwen came up to my counter, so I said, "Howdy, ma'am. Are you finding what all you need?"

"Well, howdy to you too, friend. I'm looking for coffee."

"Aisle four," I said, pointing back behind me.

"Do you have any ready made?"

"Yes, ma'am." I pointed over to the deli. "But it ain't the good kind," I whispered. "If you want the good kind, go around the corner to Carmen's Café. They got espresso."

"I guess you got me figured out." She smiled, flashing these fox-brown eyes at me. That's when I spied Lance beyond her tan shoulder, looking like an ice sculpture. She was over by the cigarettes, a carton of Marlborough half off the rack. I wanted to yell over and tell her to close her mouth so the flies don't get in, but I was under some kind of spell myself.

This witchy woman in white glistened from head to toe like she was covered with a layer of baby oil. Her hair had ripples in it, and I had a strong itch to reach out and run my hand over it the way I would a horse's mane.

Lance dropped the cigarette carton on the floor and then she turned too fast and ran into a cartful of closeouts. I cringed for her.

Meanwhile Gwen smiled and kind of curtsied and then swept away.

For a minute both Lance and I were mesmerized and couldn't think what to say or do. Finally Lance came to her senses and came over to me.

"Who was that mystery woman, Halley?"

"Hell if I know," I said just as lost as Lance was.

"You want to get a beer when you get off?" Lance asked, looking out toward the parking lot.

"You bet. See you at Carmen's in half an hour." Lance and I had been beer buddies for months, and a couple of times I'd had her over for supper with me and my kids. I felt sorry for her, at least that's what I thought I felt, 'cause she didn't have any family left in our sorry town.

By the time I made it to Carmen's, Lance had already found her way to the witchy woman. They were sitting at a small round table over in the corner. For a shy girl, Lance moved fast! She winked at me, which I took to mean, *Back off, sister.* So I took a stool up at the counter and ordered me a draft. I couldn't stay long though 'cause my kids would be getting home from school. I acted like I was reading the classifieds, but really I was listening with my superior hearing for what was going on at that table for two.

I heard Gwen talking about the full moon coming up tomorrow night. "The moon has a cosmic voice all her own," she was telling Lance. "Every full moon I answer her call and dance naked and howl like a she-wolf."

I heard Lance laugh and then cut the laugh off like she'd just gotten real serious.

"Back home my friends come out and dance with me."

"Where's home?" I heard Lance ask.

"Joshua Tree. In the desert."

I swiveled around on my stool and spied on Lance out of the corner of my eye. I'd never seen her blue eyes so captured before. I could tell her little cowboy world was about to change—for better or for worse, I didn't know.

Me and my kids, Bess and Little Dave, had just had our tomato soup and grilled cheese sandwiches. Sounds like a lunch instead of a supper, but it's what we all wanted. The kids had gone into the TV room to watch "Bewitched," and I was at the sink when I heard a little *rap rap* on my back door.

"Come in!" I yelled, thinking it was the kids' dad who I divorced the year before. That's why I was surprised to see Lance standing in my kitchen with her cowboy hat in her hand. She looked so bashful it just about broke my heart.

"Well, sit on down here, Lace—I mean Lance." (I did that on purpose 'cause I still liked Lace better.) I dried my dishwater hands on a towel and said, "You want me to make you a grilled cheese sandwich?"

"No thanks, Halley." She hung her head and clutched that old hat with both hands.

"Well, what can I do for you, partner?" I motioned toward a kitchen chair, and we both sidled up to the table.

"You are the only one I can talk to," she said. "It's that woman—Gwen—she don't live around here, but she's visiting her aunt in the nursing home."

"Tell me about it, hon," I said nice and gentle, trying to make her feel at ease. Lance had only ever had a couple of short-term girlfriends and both had caused her grief.

"I feel like, aw, shit—I'm crazy about her."

Lance wasn't telling me anything I hadn't figured out myself, but the way she said "crazy about her" made me fill up with green envy. It's not like I ever thought of myself as a dyke (even though Big Dave said I looked like a cute little dyke in my Levi's and boots). It's just that I recognized that hot passion I ain't had in years and I missed it, goddammit!

Lance went on to tell me that she was scared as hell. Gwen had invited her to dance in the full moon the next night at the old cemetery outside of town. That's what Gwen liked—getting naked and dancing on graves and howling at the moon. But Lance never took all her clothes off for anyone and she was scared shitless.

"Look, Lance, you gotta follow your heart before it's too late. You know that woman ain't going to be here long and she's probably going to bust up your heart bad, but if she's got something you want, you gotta go after it."

Lance looked at me—shocked. "I thought you was going to talk me out of it. You was supposed to tell me what a bad idea it was. Ain't you got nothin' else to say?"

"Shoot, Lace," I said realizing how unlike myself I was being. Just then I saw Bess and Little Dave standing side by side in the kitchen doorway like we were a TV show they were watching. "You kids vamoose," I said, playacting I was pissed off. "This is adult talk."

"Ain't no skin off my teeth," Bess said and stomped away with Little Dave on her heels. I cringed hearing her sound like my cynical old self.

The next day at the store when Lance came in for her Red Bull and Snickers, she looked different. She still had on the same sort of cowboy clothes and the same dusty hat, but her face looked wide awake like it was expecting important news any moment and she didn't know yet whether she'd be laughing or crying.

When she sauntered up to my checkout stand I could tell she was terrified of the secret between us.

"So, what's the verdict, Lancelot?"

"I ain't decided yet," she replied, handing me a worn five-dollar bill. Her hand shook.

"I know what I'd do if I were you," I said, but the minute I said it I knew I'd made that up. At that moment I didn't know diddly about what I would have done in Lance's shoes—or cowboy boots.

That's all we managed to say before three customers with overflowing carts and kids lined up behind Lance. I latched on to Lance's icy blues as I handed her the change and tried to get her to read my mind. *Go!* I wanted to yell at her. *Get butt naked and dance on your mama's grave.*

I turned red as the catsup I was ringing up. My own thoughts shocked me—like I'd just discovered I was a lesbian after all these years—a sex-crazed one to boot.

After work I didn't have to worry over the kids 'cause they were staying at Big Dave's that night. That was a stroke of good fortune for me. I knew what I was going to do. There was no turning back.

First I went home and dug up some black Levi's and a black T-shirt. Then I pulled a black stocking cap over my head even though it was hot out. I looked in the mirror and laughed. There was a twinkle in my eye. I never thought I'd be a peeping tom, but then I can be pretty slow. At thirty-three, I felt like a teenager sneaking out of the house.

I parked my truck on a gravel road a ways off from the graveyard. I didn't want Lance to figure me out if she saw that pickup—that is, if she came, but I knew she would. She had to come, just like I had to. Somehow we'd both heard the call.

The glowing moon was already rising as I crept across a wet, muddy field with a tiny penlight so I wouldn't fall in a hole and break a leg. I had to keep from laughing—sort of an evil laugh if you ask me. Where'd that come from? I had thought Lance's world was going to turn inside out, but I didn't get it until I was creeping across that field that my world was standing on its head and was about to pitch itself out of orbit.

It took me a while to get over there, and my feet were covered in mud up to my ankles when I saw the first tombstone starting to come to life in the milky moon. I crept in closer and sat down on the base of a tall, black granite monument. I kicked off my sneakers so I could get those wet socks off.

That's when I saw Gwen emerge from the shadows. She had a bright white cape tied around her shoulders, and other than that, she was naked. I mean gloriously naked! Her breasts looked like perfect creamy moons, and her rounded belly and thighs made me think a love goddess had just fallen out of the sky. She had a serene look on her face and was saying something in a rhythm. I couldn't concentrate on the words. I was so captivated by Gwen's cosmic beauty that for a moment I almost forgot about Lance.

But then another figure emerged from the shadows. My cowboy/girl still had her hat on and a long, black T-shirt. Her pale muscular thighs stood out like white marble. Even from a distance I could feel her trembling. I was trembling too and wrapped my arms around the monument to anchor me.

There they were: the witchy woman and the cowboy/girl—face-to-face in the moonlight with tombstones sprouting up around them. I saw Gwen reach gently to take the hat off Lance's curly head. She tossed the hat like a Frisbee and it landed over by me. Then I saw Gwen take hold of the bottom of Lance's T-shirt and start to raise it ever so slowly over her head.

That's when I realized I had my hand up under my own T-shirt and was holding one of my own breasts. My goddess! I pulled off my own shirt and held both of them like I was some kind of desperate nympho. As I did that, I saw Gwen doing the same thing to Lance, and Lance was leaning her head way back like she was in a rapture over the moon.

But the moon didn't hold her long. She reached for the curve in Gwen's shimmering waistline and pulled her close, those two female bodies somehow fitting exactly right, while the moon glowed off them into my eyes.

When I saw them kiss—at first barely touching and then totally lost in each other—I knew I was done for. How the heck did I never figure out that I could be a lesbian too?

With lips locked they started to sway back and forth as though they could hear some music I couldn't, and then all at once, Gwen swung Lance around and then Lance swung Gwen around. They both laughed and then Gwen howled like a wolf, her head thrown back. Then there was another howl, but I couldn't figure where it came from.

All at once I realized that Gwen and Lance had stopped dancing and had turned facing my direction. Was it me who had howled like a she-wolf? I looked down and realized I had taken off all my clothes and was holding Lance's hat in my hand. Gwen howled again, and I answered. Then Lance howled for the first time and I answered that too.

"Halley?" Lance said.

"That's me," I said. "Is this a private party?"

"You're welcome to join us," Gwen said. She smiled like she had me figured out all along.

For a second I felt like I was attached to the ground and was going to have to uproot myself to move forward. But it didn't take me long. I didn't say another word that night, but Lance did. She stood back and looked at me like she was seeing me for the first time. "I knew it, girl. I knew it."

I danced naked on the graves in the light of the full moon with those two, and we all howled like a pack of wolves that belonged together.

The next day at the store it seemed like I couldn't do anything right and had to call the manager two or three times for over rings. It wasn't me behind that counter. Well, it was me and it wasn't. It was a new me and this new me didn't quite fit in.

I was anxious to see Lance saunter in for her usual. I didn't know what I was going to say when I saw her, and I was a little afraid I was going to grab on to her like you would a lifesaving ring if you were drowning in the lake.

When I did see her come through the electric-eye door, my breath stopped short. Lance looked totally different. Same clothes and hat, but she was beaming like the full moon. I swear there was a glorious light coming off her.

I had a whole passel of customers lined up, and for the life of me I couldn't make no small talk—just "Thanks and have a good day."

Lance waited a long time to get to the head of the line with her Red Bull and Snickers. And when we finally stood face-to-face with only the counter between us, I felt like I was blinded by the light and couldn't look at her straight on. I rang her up, she handed me the five-dollar bill, and when I went to take it, she didn't let go. I looked up into her icy blues and time came crashing to a stop. There may have been babies crying and mothers yelling, but I couldn't hear a thing.

Lance winked at me and I laughed. But inside I started crying. I suddenly worried that Lance had come inside to say good-bye. Had the Witchy Woman won her over?

"Don't go, Lance," I said, just loud enough for her to hear, and she winked at me again, let go of the five-dollar bill and smiled broad enough for the whole world to see. She had won *me* over and she was proud of it.

My life hasn't been the same after that and neither has Lance's. In fact, the next day, after Gwen drove back to the California desert alone, Lance and I went out to the graveyard and had a private dance all our own. I'd come to realize that I love Lance in a way I didn't know I could, and all along she had been waiting for me to get it.

GET THE GIRL

Jamie Schaffner

Y ou go to Buchanan, right?" The Rudy's Record clerk leaned over the counter and twisted his leather wrist-cuff. I stepped back, nodded and waited for him to search for my Blondie cassette in the stack next to the cash register. "I graduated two years ago," he said, "Whit Smithson."

I recognized the name. He'd played some minor position on the football team, but he looked like crap now.

"State champions." He flashed his ring.

"Cool. Can I get my tape?"

"It's in the back," he said. "Want to go with me?"

I crossed my arms and he shrugged, lifted up the counter and waddled toward the beaded curtain.

While my brother and sister zigzagged through the aisles and my mother flipped through the dusty discount rack, I kept my eyes level, not dropping them toward the bongs and pipes, and glanced toward the posters, where I saw Jenny standing. I gripped the display case. It was weirdly unreal, like seeing a

movie star in person. Her blonde Dorothy Hamill hair bobbed
to the music.

I'd pictured running into her hundreds of times at Fred
Meyer's, Dalton's or Rexall. I'd be casual and charming, ask her
how B-Jazzlers practice had gone, what new prom decorations
had arrived, if she'd finished her homework. I'd engage her with
an armload of nothings and when the moment was right, I'd say,
Want to get a bite to eat?

But not now. My mother was here. I lowered my head.

"Isn't that Jenny?" my brother Benny said, our sister in tow.

"Shut up," I said.

My mother flapped a Neil Diamond album at me. I shifted
and ignored her, but she sauntered over. "Natalie, look, it's
Jenny," she whispered.

I nodded, wishing futilely that this time she'd leave a stone
unturned. I'd do the laundry, set the stupid table, take out the
garbage, if she'd just let this go. She lowered her glasses and
stared at me. My clammy grip slipped on the glass counter.
What if I fainted? But that wouldn't work. In the ambulance
she'd hover over the cot yelling above the siren, "Why aren't you
talking to Jenny?"

I couldn't tell her that I didn't know how to act around
Jenny. I wasn't the same person at home as I was at school, and I
didn't want my mother to see me as the school-me, which wasn't
like anything really, but it wasn't me. The home-me wasn't me
either. When the two versions of me collided, it didn't make a
whole me, it made two fake me's, each cancelled the other out,
so there wasn't any way to be. And now that there was more
going on with Jenny, there was another me, not the easy-breezy
meaningless school-me or the home-me. I needed to be this new
other person because if I went back to the school one, even for a
second, Jenny would never be her other me with me. And which

was I supposed to be with my mother leaning over a display case of bongs in a head shop?

"Found it," Whit said and rang up my order. "Bitchin' album."

My sister gasped at the word. I thrust my money at Whit. Jenny wasn't at the posters anymore. If I could get out of there without her seeing me, everything might not be ruined.

Whit took in my family, leaned over the counter and lowered his voice. "You want to catch the laser light show?" I grabbed my bag with my cassette and turned as my mother flicked her eyes between me and the former football hero, then gave me a syrupy look like she understood everything and it was just between us girls. "We'll meet you next door."

She prodded Benny and my sister toward the exit. Whit had scrawled his number on the bag. I wanted to crumple it, but he'd gotten my mother to leave the store. I should have tipped him.

I searched through the aisles, hoping Jenny was still there but dreading finding her. She had to have seen me and heard my family stage whisper her name. How could I tell her that I ignored her because I didn't want to pretend that we were something less than we were? And I wasn't sure she was sure it was anything more. Whatever she thought it was, when I found her she stood alone, her head bowed slightly, leafing through the pop albums. Her cowlick was sticking up. I touched her shoulder. She turned, holding a Hall and Oates record.

"Love this," she said.

The closer I got to Jenny's house the shallower my breath was becoming. I had to stop twice, lay my head on my handlebars and remind myself that nothing had to happen. I didn't have to pursue her, I thought, and all the nausea went away, but so did the tingling.

The gray dusk light was fading as I coasted down Birchwood Lane and saw that her mother's car wasn't in the driveway. I ground my feet into the pedals so I wouldn't fall off my bike. I knew that I was going to do this, no matter what. I couldn't go back to feeling nothing. I was done with nothing. Even if she rejected me, it was something. I patted dry my underarms then hauled my Schwinn onto the porch. The door flew open.

"Snickerdoodles in the oven," Jenny said, and I followed her into the house. It smelled sweet, and the warm air was soothing. I closed the door, took off my jacket and went into the kitchen. Hall and Oates was playing from a boom box on the table, sounding like they were trapped inside a tunnel and happily bleating their way out.

"Cool music." I wondered how long I should wait before offering up Blondie.

"Ow, ow, ow," Jenny said. The aluminum sheet she'd been holding clattered to the floor and cookies scattered onto the linoleum. She flung the towel across the room and bent down to scrape up the mess. The inside of her forearm was red.

"You need to run water on that." I pulled her to the sink, flipped on the faucet and placed her arm under the water. "Ten minutes," I said and held on to her wrist. How long could I stand here feeling her warmth, her breath on my neck, the smell of White Shoulders and flour, while the water ran down our arms?

She looked at the cookies strewn on the floor. "I should've used the oven mitt."

I dried my hands on my jeans. "No loss. Snickerdoodles suck." I picked them up and dumped them into the trash. "Wimpy cinnamon and no chocolate."

"Those weren't for you," Jenny said and moved her hips so I could get by.

I held the empty baking tray by the towel, and looked at her, though I didn't want her to see that I was hurt.

"Yours are over there." She nodded toward the counter.

I dropped the cookie sheet onto the cooling rack and peeled back the foil from the plate: chocolate-chocolate chip cookies. I held up my prize. Her eyes were playful and her mouth crinkled into a grin that I hadn't seen before. The determined scholastic Jenny was there too, but this new Jenny had teased me and it worked.

If I took three steps across the kitchen, I could kiss her cute, smirky face. Was it insensitive to kiss her while she was nursing an injury? I put a cookie in my mouth instead. We had all night. I didn't need to rush this.

"Let me taste," she said and motioned me over with her uninjured hand. She took a bite. I hadn't expected this and wasn't sure what to do next, so I stood there, a cookie shaking in my hand, and watched her chew.

Chocolate was smeared across her cheek. She looked so lickable. With my finger, I dabbed it from her soft, warm face. She leaned into my hand and I kissed her, tasting of milk chocolate. The water was still running and her back was pressed into the enamel sink as she put her cool, wet hand around my neck. My legs trembled. I held on to the countertop.

We slid to the floor. Our knees touched. She moved a strand of my hair, her brown eyes on me, and I shivered. She saw the real me, not just the fragment of me that I gave others. This was what I'd wanted and that's why I looked away. I couldn't let her see how much I needed her to see me.

She shifted where we sat and I grabbed her wrist eagerly, with no grace. But if she stood, we'd have to start over again, recross the kissing line. I pulled her closer, then pressed my hips into her as she ran her hand along my back over my white oxford shirt. My dark hair fell onto her peach-colored face. I inhaled her White Shoulders perfume, strongest where her blonde bob stopped. I'd been fooling myself on the ride over. Rejection wasn't better than nothing. Kissing was better than nothing.

Hall and Oates trilled, and the water was still sluicing in the sink. Her high cheekbones and strong chin were tinted in shadow just for me. I wanted this to be good, but it was already great. I slid her alongside me on the cold floor and fiddled with her red blouse dotted with flour, my fingers shaking. I wasn't afraid that I didn't know what to do, though I didn't. In the movies the girl sits up and the guy pulls her shirt over her head. But how was I supposed to take off another girl's blouse? They didn't show that. It was always he-on-top-of-her or her head in his lap.

What if I went too far and Jenny never wanted to see me again? I undid a button. She had on a black bra. I took a breath. I'd pictured all of our clothes off hundreds of times, but not this in-between, halfsy place, where undergarments had so much meaning. My own stretchy sports bra was worn a faded white, purchased last season in bulk. I needed the darkening night to cover us, but the switch was across the room.

As we kissed, I let my fingers slip between the buttons and touched her satiny bra and then her warm skin. She exhaled softly. The music clicked off.

"I need to turn off the water." Jenny bolted up, closed the tap and left the kitchen.

I pulled my knees into my chest, my butt on the hard floor. The bathroom door closed. I waited hopelessly, knowing it was over. It wasn't like she was going to come out wearing a negligee. If she had it would've freaked me out. I needed her to be willingly ambivalent; instead, she was decisively unwilling.

"You can stay, but…" Jenny said, opening the bathroom door. She trailed off as she tied the strings on her salmon-colored sweatpants. I stood still in front of her as if any movement would be deadly. But I needed to say something that would change her mind as she looked at me from the door. If I'd kissed her, it might not have ended, but I moved aside and let her out.

My Nikes squeaked in the hardwood hallway as I grabbed my backpack and walked out into the chilly night air. The dead-bolt clicked behind me. I'd left my chocolate-chocolate chip cookies inside.

I'd pictured this in hundreds of ways, and in none of them was I riding my bike home forty-two minutes after getting to Jenny's. I was supposed to stay the night! I adjusted my back-pack and threw my hood over my head. The drizzle speckled my coat and skated off my icy blue Schwinn. The light in her bedroom went on. I switched on my headlight as I pedaled down her driveway onto the slick street.

My tires sloshed through puddles and water cascaded over my pants. This couldn't be completely over, it had barely begun. Only a minute ago, she'd looked at me with that look. And not just tonight but at the railroad tracks too. A purposeful, nonfriendship, lingering look. She knew we'd never talk about boys and French-braid each other's hair.

I braked, straddled the Schwinn at the end of our cul-de-sac and wiped the rain from my face. I couldn't go home this early, my mother would grill me. I turned the handlebars and coasted down Mapleleaf Way.

Pedaling quickly past Jenny's street, I knew that nothing would be the same. I slowed down at the four-way stop and checked for cars. My underwear was damp and cool.

I smacked the wet leaves on the maple tree as I rode under its overhang in front of the house with the Jesus fish flag. From now on masturbating would be lame. Being turned on by someone else was much more exciting than what I could do to myself. I was pathetic, seventeen years old and just figuring out lust. A car flashed its lights. I flipped the driver off and veered to the edge of the road. The wind gusted, and I smelled White Shoulders.

I locked the bike outside Fred Meyer's, shook out my wet jacket, and remembered how I had told myself that once I got to college I'd find a guy that made me feel something, but now I thought it wasn't just the provincial Portland boys that were the problem. As I passed by the cashier in her green apron, she waved. I was getting to be a regular Saturday night visitor.

Standing in front of the magazine rack, I flipped through *Glamour*—ads for makeup and quizzes about finding your ideal boyfriend. I stopped on an article that talked about achieving an orgasm. You were supposed to shift your body so the man's penis would stimulate your clitoris. I put the magazine back and finished reading *Rage of Angels*.

My body warm from sitting in Fred Meyer's, I wasn't prepared for the wall of wind on the uphill ride home. Only a half mile to go, but my hands were already numb and my ears stung. My cheap headlight needed new batteries. The faded yellow blotch only lit up a few feet of the dark street. I pedaled harder. Inches from overtaking it, I was going faster than the speed of light! If the impossible could happen, then time travel was also real. I'd go back to Jenny's and start over from when she burnt herself on the Snickerdoodles. But what could I do or say that would keep her kissing me?

As I turned onto Mapleleaf Way a car slowed behind me. I swerved into the soft mud shoulder and waved it on, but the asshole wailed on the horn. I craned my neck, squinted into the lights and magnanimously displayed the bird, but my breath cramped in my chest, hoping this wasn't a pack of boys out on the prowl. Then my eyes adjusted, and I dropped my hand.

The Sherman Tank's door swung open, the dome light went on and my mother got out. Benny was in the passenger seat wearing green flannel pajamas. I hopped off my bike and my backpack slid down my shoulders.

"Where've you been?" my mother said as she charged toward me. "And don't say Jenny's." The Sherman's headlights cast a misty glow around her white parka with a fur collar.

I dropped my head, stared at the goopy muck. I couldn't tell her anything. Not about the confounding end of such close contact. Not that I was killing time at Fred Meyer's to avoid coming home obnoxiously early. And especially not that someone had seen the real me. Even though it was too brief, would never happen again and worried me when I thought about what it meant, it was by far the best thing that had ever happened. I wished she could've known that.

"Just go home," my mother said and got back into the car. The Sherman trailed behind me as I biked through the bone-white tunnel of its headlights. When we got home I'd admit that Jenny and I got into an argument, and I went to Fred Meyer's. But I couldn't think of a plausible reason why I didn't just come home.

I turned onto our cul-de-sac. The neighbor's witch hazel stunk like charred lamb. I'd say nothing. My mother couldn't prove anything. She could ground me until I left for college, but in ninety-one days, I was free from this state: the stifling rain and my hovering family.

The garage door rolled up as I turned into the driveway. I put the Schwinn away and went inside, but my mother grabbed my shoulder before I could get into my bedroom.

"Natalie, don't think I don't know what's going on," she whispered at a yell, so she wouldn't wake my father. Her body shook as if it was vibrating with the withheld volume.

I clenched my backpack strap and forced myself not to step into my bedroom. How did she figure it out? Had she seen how excited I was when I left the house and now she saw the difference? I knew she had no concrete evidence. I'd been careful not to use "she" or "her" and scrambled the meaning of my poems when writing them in my spiral notebook.

"Jenny called," my mother said and moved closer to me, standing in the hallway.

My hand started shaking. I shoved it into my pocket and tried to blink casually. My mother's eyes flitted behind her glasses, which happened when she was furious.

Benny stood behind my mother, gaping at the interrogation.

"You were with that boy from the record store," she said.

"Jenny told you that?" I pressed my back into the wall.

My mother sent Benny upstairs.

"No, but she wanted to know if you were here." My mother shoved her finger into my chest. "Which means you weren't there."

I was trying to keep up with what my mother did and didn't know. She crossed her arms and waited for me to explain. I didn't have enough time to figure out why Jenny had called, but I knew it wasn't to tell my mother that we'd been kissing. I cleared my throat and because it was the safest thing to do, I'd lie.

Protecting us both from the truth, I started to tell her the most make-believable teenage story about a girl who secretly meets the former football hero at Rudy's Record Shoppe, but I couldn't get the words out. I was crying.

My mother reached for me. I bristled and covered my face. I never let myself cry in front of her. Now I was sobbing, mucus bubbled from my nose. I wiped my face with my coat sleeve.

She fished out a travel-sized Kleenex pack from her purse and touched my shoulder with it. Her eyes stopped flickering and softened in pain. I tried to stop my tears and let her comfort me, but I couldn't. The tears pooled on my chin. I'd never be what she wanted. No matter who I kissed, I'd always be the misfit daughter in pants, no makeup and scruffy hair who liked to sit in the living room talking with the men, not in the kitchen cutting vegetables with the women. She didn't want to comfort the real me, she wanted to soothe the distorted mirror me, which in this moment, I couldn't find and reflect.

"You're such a smart kid, but such a dummy about this kind of thing," my mother said and unzipped her coat. "Don't worry, I'm not telling your father."

I nodded.

"You scared the crap out me." She tossed her keys into her purse. "There are all kinds of meshuggahs out there who can hurt you."

I blew my nose. I'd scared the crap out of *myself,* I thought. How could she not know I knew it was stupid to be riding around alone at night? I'd been living with the queen of fear for seventeen years. If I was six minutes late coming home from Steiny's, I pictured my mother pacing in the kitchen, staring at the oven clock until I got home.

"In a few months I won't be able to protect you." Her voice cracked. Now, she was crying.

I held out the Kleenex. She grabbed my hand and hugged me. "You know that your father and I are proud of you, right?" she said into my ear. The fur on her parka tickled. I hugged her back.

She let me go and the fur collar sagged around her shoulders. "Next time, bring that record boy back here to meet us," she said as she headed up the stairs. She stopped on the steps, turned and looked at me. "Call Jenny." She pushed up her glasses. "She's worried about you, too."

I hauled the phone across the den, yanked the cord so that it reached into the bathroom, locked both doors and sat on the cold toilet seat.

"Natalie?" Jenny said, picking up on the first ring.

"Yeah," I said and then ran out of ideas of what to say next.

"What happened?"

I wanted to ask her the same thing. Why weren't we still lying on the kitchen floor wrapped in each other's arms? I thought, but I knew she meant after I'd left her house. I twisted the spiral cord around my hand and told her how my mother's innate homing device tracked me down. I paced from the shower to the sink and forced myself to relax. It was useless to worry about what she might have wanted or to wish that she wanted more than she did.

"I didn't mean to get you in trouble," Jenny said.

"It's cool." I stopped in front of the mirror. A zit was forming on my forehead. "I cried so I wouldn't get grounded."

"I wish I could tear up on cue."

"I have hidden talents." I held the phone with my shoulder and popped the pimple.

"Since you're not under lock and key," Jenny said, "come over again."

I grasped the receiver. I wanted to, but if she pulled away again, this time I wouldn't be able to hide the pain. And if she didn't stop us, there'd be no denying what I was. A tunnel of wind buzzed between us.

"It won't happen again," she said.

I slid to the bathroom floor. While she hadn't said anything there was always the possibility of something. The unknown was better than nothing. "My mother needs to use the phone," I said.

"Wait," Jenny said. "I meant I won't be so mean."

I held the phone away from my mouth and breathed out.

"You there?" she said. "I need to see you."

"The Mossad agent won't let me out." I stood and brushed at the wrinkles on my shirt. "You come here."

I'm a lunatic, I thought, as I raced into the den and clunked the phone onto the shelf. My mother had bionic hearing, so I wouldn't be able to open the sliding glass door and let Jenny in. Maybe she could hoist herself up through my window.

I tiptoed upstairs and peered into my parents' bedroom. My father was asleep closest to the door. My mother jolted up, reached for her glasses on the nightstand and tromped into the hallway in her powder-blue nightgown and felt slippers.

"Jenny's coming over," I said.

My mother stared at me over her glasses.

"Urgent girl talk," I said, telling the truth.

She smirked with tacit approval. I knew she thought that Jenny and I were going to babble endlessly about the boy from Rudy's and this gave her joy.

"I'll wait outside," I said, "so the bell won't wake up Dad."

She patted my shoulder and went to bed. Finally, I was like the other girls.

The Buick's headlights were coming down our street. I hated that car, an occasional loaner from Jenny's father that was supposed to prove that he still loved her, but it only reminded her that he was on vacation with his new family. Jenny pulled into the driveway and cut the engine.

I ran down the porch steps then stopped, not wanting to seem too eager. After a few minutes I crept forward to see what was taking so long. Jenny was grasping the steering wheel. If she was changing her mind again, I wouldn't let her go home.

I marched around to the passenger's side and got in. The car reeked of cigars, and I'd sat on a squeaky toy.

"Just come inside," I said. "We'll, I mean we won't have to…"

She turned toward me. "We will." Her hand was shaking as she reached to touch my face and her eyes were wide, asking me to make it all okay. I realized she was more scared than I was. I leaned into her damp hand and nodded as if I was wise and then did the only thing that seemed right—I kissed her.

She shifted out from under the steering wheel, held on to me strongly and kept kissing me, tasting of strawberry Lip Smackers. Her face was smooth. I wanted to fall back onto the vinyl seat, go with her conviction, but now, I was the one who stopped us. I had to; my mother was listening for the front door.

When I pulled back, Jenny dropped her head, confused. I wanted to flounce her Hamill bob. The windows were steamed up. "Let's go in the house," I said and snagged her overnight bag.

As we walked up the steps her hands dangled, so touchable in the orangey mist from the porch light. I stayed close, reached around her and opened the door. Inside, she waited for me to latch the deadbolt. I knew she knew that if we didn't let too much distance get between us, it would be easier to go where we were going. I glanced upstairs, dimmed the hall sconce and kissed her quickly, feeling her smile as I followed her downstairs into my bedroom.

I set her bag on the lime-green carpet, horrified by the klieg-like intensity from the pendant lamp above my desk, but I didn't turn it off. That would've ruined it, making the darkness louder than the light. We could no longer pretend it was an accident, but it had to be blurry, without daunting definition.

I shut the door with my foot, listening for the click of the handle, and wished I'd chucked the piles of clean laundry from the extra bed into the closet. I gripped Jenny's waist as she leaned toward me. Her lips pressed into my mine. There was no going back. If this didn't work out, I knew our friendship was over, but I didn't care as her hand fluttered down my arm and she hooked her fingers into my belt loops. I urged her toward my twin bed.

She squinted. "Can we kill the light?"

I let go of her, crossed the room and flicked off the switch. Kissing, we dropped onto the bed, me on top, then her on top, and then we tumbled onto the carpet. Mercifully, Jenny laughed. It seemed impossible that I could like her even more than before, but I did. Her flawless teeth shone in the dark. This was going to more than work out.

The small space between the beds was less dangerous, not laden with meaning. Jenny was pillowy and curvy as we rocked and rubbed against each other. When we rolled around on the floor, it didn't feel like rolling around on the floor.

I thought about putting my desk chair against the door. It wouldn't keep my mother out, but it would rattle, warn us if she came in. Then Jenny raked her nails across my back, and I wanted my whole body to burn like that.

Her soft neck smelled sweetly, faintly of White Shoulders. I worked off my shoes and kicked them under the bed. Jenny shifted. My knee fell between her legs and as I looked up, catching her gaze, the ceiling creaked. I put my finger over her mouth, though she wasn't making any noise. She sat upright. Our knees touched, and I hoped she wouldn't move away. The toilet flushed, the ceiling squeaked again and then, silence.

Jenny gaped upward, her eyes tight. It would be safest if we just stopped, but I couldn't, we might never get back here, so I pulled the comforter from my bed and threw it over our heads, making her laugh. I patted her cowlick and her eyes crinkled as we sat under this ridiculous tent like two ten-year-olds pretending to be camping. I shrugged, giving in to the obvious. We weren't going to do this, not tonight. Then Jenny looked at me, took in all of the real me, and this time I didn't look away. She wasn't scared of me; she didn't blink. Then she unzipped my jeans.

REBOUND

Charlotte Dare

I had the best sex of my life with a widow I met at church bingo. That's right, I said sex, church bingo and widow all in the same sentence, but before you go, "Ewww," let me explain. Leslie wasn't your grandmother's bingo widow. She was just forty-eight when her partner died three years earlier. Forget blue hair and flabby arms—Leslie wore a sexy, cropped, honey-blonde 'do, her arms toned and tanned by the summer sun.

My best friend and the bingo boss, Jan, set the ball in motion when she popped up in a Facebook instant chat. *Come on, Vanessa,* she wrote, *come to bingo tonight. It'll get you out of the house and your mind off what's her name.* She had been harping on me for weeks to come down to the church hall, dangling the carrot of this allegedly attractive older woman who played faithfully each week.

Her name is Patty, I typed back.

I know what her name is, she wrote. *Just come down. You'll have fun.*

I was tired of pacing my apartment, of trying to make sense of the last tangled year of my life—the first six months a rapid deterioration of my eight-year relationship with Patty and the last six trying to adjust to life without her. I had recently watched Jim Carrey's film, *Yes Man,* and found the idea appealing that saying yes to everything people ask might somehow lead to an exciting reversal of fortune.

FINE. I typed it in all caps to emphasize my exasperation. *I'll see you there.*

After I purchased my regular bingo slips, the mystery bonanza slip and the red bonus one, Jan showed me exactly where to sit so I'd have an optimum view of Leslie. I plunked down in a metal folding chair and arranged my purple dabber, bingo slips, leather purse and hooded sweatshirt and then took a swig of a Dunkin' Donuts decaf. Moments later, Jan texted me: *Look at the lady in line w/black sleeveless shirt & blond hair. That's Leslie.*

I spotted her instantly among the throng of thick eyeglasses, canes and white sweaters. She seemed to know everyone as she chatted her way through the snaking line. I glanced over at Jan and wiggled my eyebrows in approval.

Leslie sat across from me in her usual seat with her friend, a silver-haired queen in pointy reading glasses. I tried not to stare, but I couldn't help it. I used to fantasize about being with an older woman, never having enjoyed the pleasure. One look at Leslie and the fantasy sprang to life with renewed vigor. It got to be a game that evening—would I be able to avert my eyes each time she sensed me staring at her from the next table? Truth be told, I didn't really try that hard not to stare.

This went on for several weeks: me staring, letting her catch me for a moment, offering her an innocent smile she always returned. Leslie was safe, a rebound crush helping me realize it was possible to have some semblance of feelings for another human being again.

By the fourth week, when the crowd had dissipated during intermission, Leslie snuck up from behind and sat in the empty chair beside me. "I know you're Jan's friend, but do I know you from somewhere else?"

I shook my head, rather chagrined. "Why do you ask?"

"Well, I notice you stare at me a lot, and I just wanted to make sure I hadn't met you before and forgotten."

Snagged. "Uh, no, we haven't met before."

"Oh," she said, waiting for an explanation but too polite to ask.

"I'm sorry for being rude and staring. I just think you're very attractive." I couldn't believe I had actually told her the truth.

"Oh." She paused and then arched an eyebrow. "Are you flirting with me?"

Now I just plain felt like an ass. There I was sitting in a church hall at a bingo fundraiser for a Catholic school being called out for leering at a widow—by the widow. But I stuck with honesty in light of my surroundings. "I guess I am. I mean you are very hot, but I never meant to make you feel uncomfortable. I can move my seat if you want me to."

She smirked, caught up in the intrigue. "You think I'm hot? Do you know how old I am?"

I shrugged. "Hotness has no expiration date. Ever see that photo of Helen Mirren in her orange bikini?"

She smiled again, this time with teeth. As she stood up, she patted my hand with tanned, bejeweled fingers. "And no, I don't want you to move your seat."

I was flying high on flirtation euphoria for the rest of the night. I'm sure I missed dabbing some called bingo numbers, but the fifty-dollar prizes were no longer of primary interest.

* * *

The following week was the last I would be able to see Leslie. I was taking a fall course at the community college that ran on Tuesdays, same night as bingo. So I sauntered into that church hall brazenly, egged on by both the hint of encouragement Leslie had given me the previous week and a heaping load of *nothing to lose.* From my usual seat, I monitored the entrance for Leslie, my heart racing faster the closer the clock ticked toward seven.

She made a point of smiling and saying hello to me when she arrived, and for the next hour and a half, my eyes lingered recklessly on her.

During intermission, as Leslie's friend went to the kitchen for a cup of coffee, she sat alone stretching against the back of the metal chair.

"Mikey, come here," I called out to Jan's eight-year-old as he milled around, looking for something to do. "Do me a favor and go give this to Leslie." I handed him a folded up losing bingo slip.

He hesitated. "Why do you want me to give it to her?"

"Don't worry about why." I waved the second-half bingo slips in his face. "I'll let you play some of my cards after break."

I watched Leslie from the moment Mikey left my side. When he walked over to her, she flashed him a bright smile. After reading the note, she glanced at me, refolded the slip and stuck it in her purse with a nod, amused in spite of herself.

Sitting on Leslie's couch a week later, I glanced around her living room, peering into this stranger's life through the photos over her fireplace—her nephew's graduation, a group shot of friends from a ski vacation and a particularly gorgeous one of her and her dead partner on some beach at sunset. Nice. Eerie but nice. She had surprised me when she called and said yes to my scribbled dinner invitation, but even more surprising was the natural flow of dinner conversation earlier that evening. We joked and laughed, exchanged views on various issues from healthcare reform to easy, last-minute cocktail party snacks. But my favorite part of dinner was Leslie's rosy-faced grin when I told her the bingo hall fluorescents had belied her real beauty.

Now, while she poured us glasses of pinot grigio in the kitchen, my imagination wandered off in all sorts of directions. I spotted her stereo remote and tuned the radio to the AM station that plays American standards. The Glenn Miller Orchestra's "Moonlight Serenade" had set the mood by the time Leslie sat down with the wine.

"What do you think, I'm seventy years old?" she asked with a smile and handed me my glass.

I laughed. "Who says I put this station on for you? I love this music."

She leaned back against the couch, her arm brushing past mine. "I usually listen to Top Forty, but this is perfect for a relaxing evening. It reminds me of when I was a kid at my Nonna's house on Ferry Street in New Haven."

"I had a grandmother who lived in New Haven, too."

"Every Italian kid did. I think it was the law," she said, playing with the ends of her hair.

I smiled at the one thing that didn't seem to accentuate our age difference, and then indicated a large, three-wick candle on the coffee table. "Can I light this?"

She nodded. "Well, this isn't that different so far," she said, referring to our dinner conversation in which she revealed she hadn't been on a date since meeting Rita two decades earlier.

"The way people go about getting dates may have changed in the last twenty years, but the date itself is still pretty standard." I clicked off the lamp and then sat back, not sure what to do next. It occurred to me that I had never seduced an older woman before. Actually, I'd never seduced anyone before, and I suddenly froze with awkwardness.

"So Vanessa, what's next on your agenda this evening?" She sipped her wine and her lips shined deliciously after she licked the excess off them.

Looking straight ahead, I said, "Well, I was going to try to kiss you once I got up my nerve."

"Oh." She dropped a wicker-wedged flip-flop to the floor. "And how long does that usually take?"

I laughed quietly, stuffing my hands between my buttcheeks and the sofa cushions to conceal their trembling. "Not this long, but you're not my usual date. You're amazing, Leslie. Fun, sophisticated, enchanting."

"Thank you." She sighed deeply. "You know, it's been a long time since someone looked at me, I mean really looked at me."

"I can't believe no one's moved in on you yet. What's the matter with these women?"

She laughed and absently patted my thigh. "It's funny. After Rita died, I couldn't imagine being with anyone for the longest time. But if someone told me that three years later I'd be sitting here with a woman eighteen years younger, I would've said they were nuts."

"The first night I saw you at bingo I never dreamed I'd be here either—well, I did dream about it, but I never really expected it would happen."

Her gaze halted my breath for a moment as I realized I was feeling more than just the urge to jump on her. As badly as I desired her, I could've simply sat there all night watching the shadows from the flickering candle flames dance across her face.

"So you wouldn't mind if I kissed you?" I finally asked.

She playfully contemplated the question. "I don't think so."

"Okeydokey then." I took Leslie's wineglass and mine and placed them on the coffee table.

"Your hands are shaking," she said and clutched them in hers. They were warm; her grip firm, purposeful.

I pulled them back. "You make me nervous."

To my surprise, she reached out and caressed my cheek. "You make me nervous, too."

Suddenly, her hand gently pulled my face toward hers. When our lips made contact, I took over, taking it slow with long, sensual kisses. She giggled as I tickled her lips with the tip of my tongue, and my pussy tingled when she snuck her tongue into my mouth. As my kisses grew more aggressive, she moaned, tracing my triceps with her hands.

"Are you okay?" I whispered.

"Yes," she whispered back, wrapping both hands around the back of my neck.

I nudged her back against the arm of the couch and crept on top of her, wedging my thigh between her legs. Her arms slide down to my back, her fingers stroking me through my shirt as I devoured her mouth with hard kisses and a determined tongue.

She gripped my ass and pushed me into her. I couldn't believe what I was feeling. She was completely into it.

I kissed her cheek, her chin and then her neck, whirling my tongue lightly under her ear. When I started sucking her earlobe, she writhed with pleasure, and I gushed with wetness.

"Oh, Vanessa."

"I hope I'm not being too pushy." I was unsure of the protocol involved in luring a widow back into the saddle.

"I don't care," she breathed. "I'm very turned on right now."

Taking her cue, I unbuttoned her blouse, kissing her from the neck down, gliding my tongue between her warm breasts. Her breathing escalated as my lips trailed down the middle of her torso, stopping at the waistband of her Capri pants. She moaned as I tugged at the fastener with my teeth, but I wasn't ready to seal the deal just yet.

Kissing my way back up to her breasts, I unhooked her bra and stroked her nipples as I nibbled her lips. Her hands ravaged me, squeezing the flesh on my back and mussing my hair, running her fingers through it.

"I haven't felt this good in so long," she murmured as I tongued her hard left nipple and tweaked and twisted her right one. "Vanessa, I want you."

She pulled off my shirt and hugged my hot skin against hers. I teased her neck, licking and sucking, letting her body's undulations guide me. She began grinding her crotch against my upper thigh in a rhythm I felt against my clit, already throbbing wildly.

"Leslie," I warned, "if you keep doing that, you're going to make me have an orgasm."

"I want you to touch me." Her hot breath dampened my ear.

I opened her pants, stuck my fingers in and played around in her wetness. She whimpered again and squeezed me tighter, squirming against my hand.

"That's not how I want to have you." I slowly rolled down her pants and spread her legs, diving down on her.

"Oh, my god," she said as I slid my tongue inside her and swirled it around. I teased her clit, flicking and sucking it as her moans reached a fever pitch. After a few moments, she grabbed my head and tried to keep me in place. "Baby, I can't hold back anymore."

I glided two fingers inside, fucking her vigorously as my tongue riveted her clit, whipping her into a climax that had her shrieking, clutching the sofa cushions. She came with a force that seemed to purge three years of grief and loneliness. After her body stopped shuddering, I climbed up and kissed her neck softly.

"I've never come so hard," she said, still gasping for breath.

"It's been a while, huh?"

"Too long." She stroked my back with her fingertips and grew quiet.

I knew what she was thinking—or rather who she was thinking about. Suddenly feeling like an interloper, I let her have the moment.

"Do you want me go?" I finally said.

She picked my chin off her chest and shook her head with a sweet smile. "I want you to stay with me. Let's go upstairs."

We gathered our clothes and went to bed but got very little sleep that night.

Leslie hadn't returned the three messages I'd left her after our weekend together. I intended to drive to her house and confront her like an adult but ended up doing the stalker drive-by instead. I had done something very stupid. Having sex with a grieving widow? No, falling in love with one.

On my fourth or fifth pass by the front of Leslie's house, I saw her walk into the kitchen. Seconds later, my cell phone started singing.

It was Leslie's home number. "Ah, shit," I muttered before answering.

"Vanessa, why do you keep driving by my house?" Her cold voice chilled me in the autumn air slipping in through the half-open window.

"You haven't returned any of my calls."

"Did you just pull into my driveway?"

"Yes. I want to talk for just a minute."

"That's not a good idea right now."

"Then when? You've ignored me for two weeks, Leslie. I know our time together meant something to you. If I was just a sport fuck, you wouldn't have asked me to stay."

She sighed, and I clicked off the call as I bounded up her front steps.

When she opened the door, her expression was less than receptive. "Come in, but it's late and I have to work tomorrow."

"I know." I closed the door and leaned against it. She propped herself against the arm of her sofa, arms folded and body well out of my reach. "Look, I get that you don't want to see me anymore, but why wouldn't you even call me back to tell me? That really hurt."

"I'm sorry, but you know why."

I decided I could be a hard-ass too. "Maybe I'm a masochist, but I just want to hear it from your lips."

Her mouth twitched defiantly. "Don't sell yourself short. You're also a little bit of a sadist."

Why did I find bitchy so irresistibly sexy? I held my ground. "Oh, I'm a sadist because I won't let you take the cowardly way out."

"Out of what? We had a great night together but that was it."

My heart sank. I knew that wasn't it, but she was running from the topic like a whore in a Vice raid.

"Look," she continued, her voice softer as she let down her defenses, "I'm just not ready to feel this level of intensity for someone, especially for someone so much younger. I didn't call you back because I was afraid if I heard your voice, I'd tell you to come over."

My mind raced. While I was skulking past her house, I

had prepared myself to walk away from this with dignity, but looking into her sparkling, pooling eyes, I lost all grasp of reason. "Leslie, this was last thing I expected too, but I can't stop thinking about you."

She slumped down onto the sofa cushions and stared into her lap. "It'll pass."

"Really? Is that the attitude the broken-hearted are supposed to take toward life?" I waited for a response, but she wouldn't look up. "I know your partner passed away and even though I can't imagine that pain, I do know about loss. I know what it feels like to believe you'll never be able to feel anything for another person again."

Frustration simmered. I felt like I was scolding a child as she sat silently, twirling the rings on her middle fingers with her thumbs.

"Leslie," I said sharply, startling her. "Tell me to go. Tell me to piss off and I'll leave you alone."

She slammed her fist sideways into a puffy throw pillow. "Damn it. Why do you have to be so wonderful...and so young?"

I sighed and plopped down beside her, quiet for a moment. "After losing Rita, I would think you wouldn't want to let anything wonderful in life pass."

She sniffled in a deep breath and swirled her fingertips around the top of my hand. "You make me feel alive again, Vanessa. I don't know what I think about that just yet."

I thumbed away a tear that escaped down her cheek. "I don't know what I think about anything these days. I just know I love being with you."

Her head fell like a feather against the back of the sofa. She was silent for a long moment before exhaling and contorting her eyebrows playfully. "I should warn you—when I fall, I fall hard."

"I can't imagine anyone I'd rather have land on me."

"What if your ex decides she wants you back?" She giggled as I tickled her forearm with my fingernails.

"She won't." I lightly kissed her neck. "She's moved on to better things."

"What a fool," she said in a breathy groan.

As I flicked my tongue behind her ear, I whispered, "What if you decide you don't want to see me again after I leave?"

"Then don't leave." She yanked me by the shirt until we fell back, our lips meeting.

She never did make it to work on time the next day. But since our wedding three months ago, I'm much better about letting her out of bed in the morning. Well, most mornings.

THINGS
I MISSED

Kathleen Warnock

If you can believe it, we used to go to church together. We'd catch the five o'clock Mass on Saturdays, which counted as the Sunday obligation, and then go out and have dinner and a few drinks. We also went on holy days, calling each other up to remind ourselves that it was the Feast of the Immaculate Conception or All Saints' Day.

This was in the Deep South in the early to mid-1980s. There weren't many Catholics in town. Sometimes we'd go to the church near the university, where she worked, or the one toward the eastern end of town, where I worked at the newspaper.

I was twenty-three, and it was my first "away from home" job. She was twenty-eight, and it was her first Division I job. I went to interview her when she was hired to head up the newly formed women's soccer team (considered rather daring, if not crazy in the mid-'80s). It was the Catholic thing that started the friendship; she said she'd been so busy she hadn't had time to find a church, and her mom kept calling her to see if she was going to Mass.

"I have a mom like that," I told her and offered to take her to the 11:00 o'clock at Our Lady of the Valley. She grinned and said she'd appreciate it, and suddenly we were two people with a bond, deep in a foreign land, surrounded by Baptists and Methodists, a few Episcopalians and the occasional snake handler. She was from the mountains of the West, and talked about how much she missed them. I was from Philadelphia and was counting the days until I could move up the newspaper food chain and one day be the beat writer for the Phillies.

She was big, like her mountains: a bit over six feet tall, with short, curly blonde hair. She held your eyes with an honest, trustworthy gaze. Spoke in calm, measured tones. I liked to get her to laugh, because she was so serious and focused. She was deeply tanned, and it made her sharp blue eyes stand out. She liked to wear T-shirts with the university logo and baggy shorts, and her long, brown legs were muscled and smooth. At home she went barefoot, and she often kicked her shoes off at the office, padding around at the athletic center on the carpet woven with the school colors. When she was with the team on the field, cleats added another inch or so to her height.

Sometimes I'd go over to the athletic center to meet her for lunch, or she'd swing by our office, which wasn't far from the university's conditioning center. She took me over there once to show me around and demonstrated how to use the Nautilus machines and free weights. She did many reps of great weights until she glistened.

The newspaper I wrote for was owned by a local family and most of the higher-ups had gone to the university, and they knew each other and scratched each other's backs and didn't print the embarrassing stuff, and rooted for the football team and to a lesser extent, the basketball team, to win. No one minded that I went for drinks with Lise, or that we went to parties at each other's houses, or when I hitched a ride with her to away games.

I had several friendships like that: with the dark-haired stringer who'd played high school hoops, and who I drove to Charlotte to help look for an apartment when she got a gig on the *Observer*. I wanted to tell her how much I'd enjoyed working with her and how I'd miss her. I had the words right in my mouth, but somehow they never came out. Then there was the graceful, model-pretty forward on the women's volleyball team. She was so kind and humble, and she introduced me to her parents, and they had me out for a barbecue, and I met her nieces and nephew. And there was the softball catcher who both terrorized and fascinated me. Her swagger was mesmerizing, and every time she saw me at a local watering hole, she'd come over and tease me and take a sip of my "girlie drink" and insist on walking me to my car for safety. She always said she'd go to Hollywood and be a stuntwoman.

I had a degree in modern languages, a couple of writing prizes and a draft of a sci-fi novel featuring two young women heroines, with a deep and complex friendship. Oh, and I hadn't a clue.

But I had some fun. I was on my own for the first time; living in a young, partying town; and I got to drive all over the countryside and go to lots of games and got paid for writing about them. And I had some good friends.

I left before Lise did—gave up the newspaper business and moved back up North to go back to school and lose myself and find myself and throw myself into causes that kept me from having a personal life, and to drink and party some more. I was quite sure that the answers I sought were just ahead. I tried to stay in touch with my old friends. We didn't have the Internet then. We wrote letters, every now and then, and placed long distance calls on phones that had cords that went into the wall.

Fast-forward five years. It's the turn of the last decade of the century. I still have lots of intense friendships with women. A few of them challenge me, and I assert my heterosexual credentials, even though they've only been used once or twice. Fast-forward another five years. The bitch of my life finally calls me on it. She taunts and harangues and seduces me out of the closet, then laughs at my ass when I declare my love for her. And at thirty-seven…I don't go to church anymore. I kind of miss it. But I don't miss the effort it took to remain in the dark all those years.

The dark-haired stringer came out to me a few years after I left the South; the model-pretty forward is twice married and a mother; the softball catcher went to Hollywood and became a stuntwoman.

And Lise… We stayed close the first few years, and she had some success with the team, got them ranked, got some national attention. Then she left. Didn't say why… I got a letter from her after she went back out West. She said she'd started working at a bank, given up coaching. I got her on the phone, and she sounded so sad. I asked her what happened, and she told me one of her players, the big star girl, head case, diva, didn't like being told what to do. Didn't think she had to follow the rules. And that cut a conservative soul like Lise to the bone. It never occurred to her that any athlete, particularly a girl athlete on a scholarship in a minor sport, would ever take her position for granted, and that she wouldn't be selfless and committed to the team and a good example to others and a role model, wouldn't do what had to be done to make a winner. That was what Lise had always been and done. And Lise decided that if the girl didn't straighten up and fly right, she'd kick her off the team. And the girl went to the athletic department and said Lise had made a pass at her.

They believed the student. There was no real investigation, just quietly ushering the tainted coach out the door for "personal reasons," "to pursue other opportunities." The school, which had had its share of scandals, with the steroids, and the grade changing and the illegal recruiting practices, was on a hair-trigger, and they felt like a dyke scandal would be the last straw. (For whom? The athletic boosters, I guess. New gyms and practice fields cost money.)

And there was Lise...who'd never dated a woman, had memorized the NCAA rulebook and would have kicked the shit out of any coach she found sleeping with a player. And she was done. Nothing official, on the record. But no one would hire her to coach again. People she'd worked with wouldn't look her in the eye, answer her calls, be seen with her. And of course, she had no one to go to church with.

So she moved back home, back with her parents and got a job in a bank, and 2,000 miles away, I cried for her. At the injustice of it all, and how even then I couldn't tell her I'd loved her. Because I wasn't there yet, either. And then we lost touch, and I often wondered about her and where she was and whether she'd ever gotten over it. Or through it. Or if she ever thought about me.

Fast-forward another ten years, and the woman asleep beside me is my love, my partner, my wife. We'll grow old together and have an interesting time doing it.

And in the last ten years, I have realized that I can either pine for all the missed opportunities of the first thirty-seven, or I can enjoy what's essentially my true adolescence, denied me back when it would have been much more difficult, and I can dream of beautiful women and making love to them, and think of what I'd say and do to the women of my dreams and fantasies, and work and play with my partner in love and mischief, the woman

who has my back (and my front) and knows what to do with
the both of them.

Of course we do have the Pandora's box of the Internet these
days, and wireless high-speed and search engines and finding
people at the touch of a button. The other night, when I was at
home alone, my laptop on my knees in bed, desperately needing
a break from a project due too soon at work, I put her name
into the browser, and in a few clicks, there she was: Lise Bender,
licensed real estate agent, serving all your residential needs. There
was a big picture of her smiling that smile, blue eyes still blazing.
Her hair had a lot of gray in it (I dye mine a shade of blonde it
never was, having finally embraced my inner femme). She had
crow's feet and laugh lines; we didn't use much sunscreen back
then. (Me? I haven't aged a day! Right.) But she was still Lise,
and my heart warmed. There was a phone number listed, but I
didn't want to jump out at her like that. So I sent her a friendly
email. Hoped she was doing well, remember me? And I gave her
my number.

Less than an hour later, the phone rang. I was back at work,
had already forgotten the email. I thought the call was from my
sweetie, telling me she was on her way home.

"Hello, love," I said. "Did you eat? Do you feel like picking
up something for dinner on your way home?"

"What? I...is this..." someone began.

"Lise?" I let out a sort of half laugh, half sob.

"Yes...yes." She sounded relieved. "I got your email and
thought...well, I hope it's not too late...I'm a couple hours
behind..."

"It's not too late," I said. "It's never too late...to talk to
you."

"I think you thought I was someone else," she began,
sounding embarrassed. "Your husband? Is he working late? Oh,

my god, it's been so long. I don't even know if you're married or not! Are you? Do you have any kids?"

"Are you? Do you?" I asked back.

"Divorced," she said. "No kids. Has it really been...?"

"A lifetime," I said. "No kids for me either. I'm with someone though. We're happy. She makes me happy." A pause. A long pause. I wondered if Lise was going to hang up. I could hear her breathing.

"So you're..."

"Happy, yeah," I agreed.

"Well, god bless ya," she said. "You can't turn that down."

"I like to think not," I said. "Have you found...?"

"Well, it wasn't my husband," she said with a sour laugh. "I don't think I've found what I'm looking for, yet. But maybe I will one of these days. At least I'm looking in the right place these days."

"Took me long enough," I said. "I was thirty-seven before I..."

"I was forty-two," she told me. "I guess we're both slow learners."

I couldn't help it. I started to laugh. In a minute, she did, too.

"Do you remember back before you left town, we went out to that Mexican place...Sancho's or Pancho's?" she began, and I knew what night she was talking about.

"Rancho's," I said. "We thought margaritas were the coolest drink *ever*...we put away a couple pitchers..."

"I don't know how we got back to your place," she said. "I was sure I was fine to drive, but we must've been plastered. They were a lot more lenient about DUI back then."

I shook my head at dumb luck, which has probably saved my ass far more times than I deserved. Somehow we'd made it back to my place, and I invited her in for a nightcap in my already-packed apartment. There were boxes all around and the pictures were off the walls, and I'd disassembled my bed and there was just the mattress on the floor.

She threw herself on it, and I crawled in next to her, and we curled up next to each other.

"I thought you were asleep," she told me, two decades and time zones later.

"I thought you were asleep," I confessed. "I wasn't."

"Neither was I."

"If I'd known..." I began. Known what?

"What would you have done?" she asked.

I thought about it. Rocky moral ground here...but I wanted her to know.

"I would have kissed you," I said, and something inside me melted. It was both incredibly sad and such a relief. "It would have been so good to kiss you, Lise."

"Yes," she said. "It would have."

"Do you know how beautiful you are?" I asked her. She sighed. "Yes. Still. And now I can tell you. This is what I would have done, Lise: I would have touched your face. I would have run my fingers through your hair, because it was so thick and bouncy. And I always wanted to touch it. And I would have held your face in both my hands and kissed you, so deep, so gently. I would have opened your mouth with my tongue, and you would have moved in closer and rolled over onto me, and I would have felt every inch of your body touching mine. And we would have taken off our clothes so we could feel each other's skin all over.

"And you would have pressed your breasts against mine, our nipples rubbing together as you rubbed your leg between mine, and you know I would have been soaking already. I always got wet when I was near you.

"And I would have taken one of your nipples in my mouth and nibbled at it, using my teeth, as you reached down and touched my clit. We were both so hot for each other, Lise. If we'd ever let ourselves know it. If we'd ever actually touched each other, we would've come in seconds. And then come again and made love all night and into the next day."

"I can see your body, plain as day right this minute," I told her. "And we would have woken up still touching, and I would have moved down to your clit and started to kiss it, and suck it, and reach deep up inside you with my fingers and my tongue, and I can hear the moans you would have made and what it would have sounded like, when you were getting ready to come, and when you came, and how you wound down afterward. I can hear it plain as day.

"It was so hot down there, remember? And I was always worried about the electric bill, so I only put on the AC when I had to. We would have been so sweaty in a few minutes, rubbing up and down against each other, slick with sweat and come and tears and kissing. Can you imagine the sounds we would have made when we touched? Sliding and groaning, reaching up and in, biting each other's lips, raking our nails down each other's back?"

I paused, aroused enough to want to touch myself. I heard Lise draw in deep, harsh breaths. I wondered if she were touching herself. Or crying. She made a sound, and it was one I had never heard from her, but I knew what it was, and it sounded familiar, because I had imagined it so many times.

"Are you all right?" I asked her. I wanted to ask her *Was it good? Was it like you thought it would be?*

"Are you?" she replied, with a catch in her voice. I knew she really was crying. "Yes. It would have been…like that."

"Well, then, that's what we would have done. Should have

done," I told her. Told myself. And I couldn't go on. We didn't say anything for a bit.

"It was really good to talk to you," she finally said.

"I'm glad I sent that email. I'm glad you called," I told her.

"Me, too." A pause. "We probably shouldn't talk again though…like this. I have a lady friend."

Same old Lise. She knew what was right and what was wrong. Whether what we'd just done constituted cheating could be debated. I didn't think I would discuss the finer points with my partner. But I didn't regret it. Couldn't happen again, though.

"Well, you know, Christmas cards. If we're passing through, kind of thing…"

"Yes, that," she agreed. "But I'm glad we…talked. It means a lot. That you said what you did. It's always something I wondered about."

"Well, then, I'm glad I could answer that for you," I told her. I heard my sweetie's key in the door.

"Good night," I said. "Pleasant dreams."

"I think I'll have some," she said, and hung up.

I wasn't sure whether to be proud or ashamed of myself. It had been so mysterious, so long ago, a permanent question mark (one of many) that had worn itself into my mind. I'd forgotten about most of them or chosen not to think of them. Pointed myself toward the future, determined not to get pulled back-ward into the darkness. It had been so lonely. But not all bad. At least I could erase that question mark. I was glad for Lise. And for me.

"I picked up something for dinner…" my partner called from the living room. "Hungry?"

"For you," I told her, hanging up the phone. It never ceases to amaze me how lucky I am.

DIRTY LAUNDRY

Cheyenne Blue

We can only talk when we're folding the sheets.

Pick up the sheet, take two corners each. Spread it out. A hard flick to straighten it. Walk toward each other, the sheet goes corner to corner.

"What's your name?"

Bend, take the bottom corners, step back, flick. Walk toward each other again, sheet goes corner to corner.

"Maura. What's yours?"

Bend, take the bottom corners, step back, flick. No need to walk toward each other this time. Sheet goes corner to corner.

"Eileen. Why you here?"

Maura bends, places the folded sheet on the pile and takes another from the laundry basket of crumpled, sun-warmed linen. She hands me two corners. "I had a baby. A little girl."

Her face is closed, shuttered, but the pain is stark in her eyes. She's only been here for two weeks; the loss is still raw, the milk still leaking from her breasts. She doesn't need to say any more;

half of the girls cloistered here in the convent have had babies out of wedlock, a mortal sin. The other half are here because, well, they're fallen women in their own way. Catholic Ireland is unforgiving of such things.

Step back, flick the sheet. Walk toward each other again, sheet goes corner to corner.

"Who has your baby?" Sometimes it's a sister or a parent who takes the child, raises it as her own, but the mother is still banished to pay for the sin of being pregnant.

Bend, take the corners, step back, flick, move toward Maura again.

"I don't know. They took her from me and told me I couldn't leave until I signed the papers."

The sentence was too long. Sister Ursula comes sweeping down and her cane cracks on the back of Maura's hand. "No talking while working."

She doesn't wait to see that we comply. We're aware of the punishment. If we don't stop talking, we'll be hauled into Mother Superior's office and then the cane will be on the backs of our bare thighs and the switches will draw blood and the cuts will chafe on our rough-spun dresses.

Maura's mouth twists and I think she's going to protest. She hasn't been here long enough to know the futility of resistance.

"No," I mouth at her.

She gives a little shake of her head and bends to take the bottom corners again. We work in silence for the next hour until the bell goes, and it's time for prayer before what passes for lunch.

I'm nineteen and I've been here for three years. I didn't have a baby, although sometimes I wish that I had, so that at least I'd have something that belonged to me, however briefly. My mother is dead, and my father is gone. My aunt unwillingly

took me in, blaming me all the time for my mother's death—
dead in childbirth with me. My aunt wasn't kind, but she wasn't
cruel. She gave me food, clothing, tuition in the faith, a toy at
Christmas and a hug sometimes—brief, hard, her face turned
away as if any emotion would make her weak—but a hug all
the same.

When I was sixteen, the parish priest started touching me.
Touching me *there*. I knew it was wrong, but you're told to
obey the word of God, so I'd stand, holding my skirts up above
my head while he stared at my exposed gee. I couldn't see what
he was doing, swathed as I was in my skirts, but I'd hear his
breathing, fast and rough, and the rustle of his hand in cloth.
And then he'd touch me with a finger, pushing it in. It stung,
but if I tried to move away, he'd drag me back and it would
sting more, so I learned to stand still. He'd finger me, and his
breathing would come faster until he groaned, and then the
finger would be gone. A rustle of cloth, then he'd say, "Put your
skirts down, you wicked girl. Go! Go!" and I'd scurry from the
room in confusion and shame.

And then one time, his housekeeper walked in as I stood
there, skirts around my ears.

I heard the door. I heard her screech of horror. I dropped my
skirts and turned around, took a step toward her. She was shaking,
her hands out in front of her, as if to ward away the devil.

"You evil, evil girl," she cried.

I glanced at the priest. He was on his feet, his cassock in
place. He crossed to me in a single stride and backhanded me
across the face. "Sinner," he spat.

My eyes skittered from one to the other. "I was only doing
what he asked," I cried.

"Liar," the housekeeper hissed. "How dare you tell untruths
in front of a servant of our Lord?"

I ran with tears of shame streaming down my cheeks. I ran all the way home to my aunt's house and, avoiding the kitchen where she sat, crept up the stairs to my bed.

The priest came the next morning and talked to my aunt. I hid upstairs, confused, not knowing what I could say to make it right. Then my aunt came into my room. "Pack your things, Eileen. You're going with the priest."

"Where?" I cried, but she wouldn't answer me, just threw some underwear and a couple of pieces of clothing into a bag and thrust it at me, turning away as the priest came and took my arm, dragging me down the stairs to his car.

And here I am.

Some of the girls have been here for many years. Some are now old women, but they still call them girls. Some are simple. Some had babies. Some are like me. We're all here to work and repent and be cleansed through hard work and discipline. Unpaid work, and the "discipline" involves cruelty you wouldn't think nuns were capable of. We're slaves. Few ever leave. Fewer ever escape.

That night, Maura is moved into my dormitory. The nuns do that. When they think you're docile enough to be with the other girls, they move you from a solitary room to the communal dorm.

Maura comes in, head down, feet dragging, her sheets and bag bunched in her hand. The other girls ignore her. It's every girl for herself. Maura hovers, unsure of where to go. I take pity on her and go over, taking her arm and leading her to the vacant bed. It's next to mine.

"Here," I say. "Sheets go on the bed. Put your things in the trunk."

Maura's eyes flicker nervously. "Thank you," she says. Her fingers pick at the cotton bag.

"Is that your clothes?" I ask.

She nods. "And a bonnet for my baby."

Forbidden.

"Don't put it in the trunk or under the mattress," I whisper. "The nuns will check. Unpick your pillow and put it inside."

She nods, although she's so passive, I don't know if she realizes what I'm telling her.

She cries that night. Stifled, gulping sobs muffled by the lumpy pillow. We all hear her, of course. I imagine her, lying face down, streams of salt soaking her pillow, her nun-cropped hair disarranged and sweaty.

I'm halfway out of my bed before I reconsider. I should leave her well alone, for her sake and for mine. My bare toes curl on the icy wooden boards. Why am I even considering this? Maura's face, all angles and lines and chapped red cheeks, swims into my vision. She needs me. We all need a friend in this feckin' place.

Before I can talk myself out of it, I'm padding across the short space to her bed. I pull back the thin cover and slide in next to her, wrapping my arm over her thin back. Her shoulder blade juts up like a chicken's wing.

"Shh," I say. "It will be all right." Meaningless, soothing nonsense. Of course it won't be all right.

But Maura turns onto her side and curls trustingly into my body, like a kitten squirming into safety. "I want my baby back," she whispers. "I should never have signed the papers."

I stroke her damp hair. Time enough later to tell her that there is no going back. Those papers are final. Others have tried, and others have failed. For now, I can only offer her comfort. My hands stroke her back, her hair, her soft, damp face.

"Sleep now, kitten," I say. "I'm here. Tomorrow is another day."

She sighs, and her fingers grasp my nightdress, curling loosely into the rough cloth. Soon, the soft exhalations tell me she's asleep.

I lie awake for a while, holding her. It's like coming home. But I know I can't stay, and in the frosty starlight through the open window, I move like a shadow back to my own bed. I can't be in her bed in the morning. The nuns are merciless for things like that.

The seasons move through time, and we go through the motions. Washing the sheets, slapping them in the sink, wishing they were Sister Ursula's face. The small, sweet pleasure of hanging wet laundry on the line on a sunny day and for brief stolen moments turning my face up to the weak sunshine and imagining I'm free. The weekly health walk to the small town, where, although we're laughed at, pointed to, titters behind hands and twitching curtains, at least we're out, in the real world, albeit for a few precious minutes.

And then there's my lifeline. Nighttime. Waiting until the lights are out, and the breathing of the other girls settles into rhythmic snorts and sighs. Waiting until the darkness is absolute and my movements hidden. I steal out of my bed, bare feet gliding cautiously over the floorboards. A step, another, and then I'm sliding into Maura's bed.

We don't talk, except in whispers, our heads under the covers. Often, we don't talk at all, we simply align our bodies together and let our hands do the talking, gestures of reassurance, of caring, of love. I'll spoon behind Maura, and my palms will smooth over her belly, smoothing away the pain from her womb, and the absence of its produce. I'll soak in the warmth and comfort of another body and let my hands convey all the love that I have. Or Maura will cradle my head on her breast and stroke my shoulders, my back, and whisper words of love into my hair.

The first time she kisses me properly, I feel the tremble of her lips on mine, their hesitancy and their sweet, chapped, feather touch. She draws back, and her whisper floats through the darkness. "I'm sorry."

My fingers settle on my own lips, reliving her kiss. "It's a sin. It has to be."

"Any more than the sins we've already committed? They said my perfect baby was a sin, and that can't be right." She kisses me again with more assurance and her fingers clutch my shoulders. "I love you, Eileen. I don't know what I'd do without you."

When she kisses me again, I kiss her back.

We have to hide our love. From the other girls, who would sell what was left of their souls if it got them a small favor from the nuns. And especially from the nuns. Although we don't know exactly why, we know that what we do, together under the cover at night, will be considered wicked. Evil. And we will be punished and separated forever. So during the days we work in silence with the rest of the girls, taking care that we are never seen together too often. We sit apart at mealtimes; we ensure that in the two-by-two weekly march to the town we always walk with a different girl. If by chance, we both are hanging wet sheets on the line at the same time, we content ourselves with a brush of fingers.

Nighttimes are our time. I learn to place my pillow down in the bed so that to the casual glance, it looks as if there's someone there. It's often so cold that most of the girls sleep with their heads under the covers, although that too is discouraged. We're supposed to have our hands visible, so that we can't be acting out our impure thoughts on ourselves. But unless a nun comes in at night—and they seldom do—there's no one to police us on that. So I get away with it. And Maura's bed is in the corner, so there's no one too close to hear our whispers or the rustle of the stiff sheet as our hands slide over each other, learning the pathways and expressions of love.

The years pass. Sister Ursula dies and inwardly we rejoice, although not for long, as her successor, Sister Monica, is younger and keener and her wrist is better able to inflict the switch on our thighs. More girls arrive, and we turn our faces to the wall so that we don't hear their cries as they plead for their babies to be brought back to them. Some girls die—consumption, flu or mysterious sickly wasting illnesses—and they are buried out in the apple orchard in unconsecrated ground. No gravestone marks their resting place. And a few girls leave when a brother or a mother or an aunt brings a letter.

I forget how old I am, but my menses become irregular. There are strands of gray in Maura's hair. But the constant of work and prayer and porridge and soup and bread with jam on Sundays continues. This is our life and now we don't think of any other. But our other life in the dark goes on, and love is our only comfort.

And then, one day, there's a lady at breakfast. She's not a nun. She wears a dress and she smiles at us. She carries a clipboard, and she says she will talk to us all by ourselves. The laundry is to be closed. She is there to find out what we want to do. Ireland has changed, she gently tells our down-bent heads. You are welcome in the community.

One girl, one brave and bold girl, raises her hand. "Can I have my little girl back now?" she asks.

There's a pause, and there's a catch in the lady's voice when she answers, "We'll try. We'll try our hardest to find out where your baby is."

She talks to us all one by one in the office. But Sister Monica is in the room, sitting malevolently by the door, a grim restricting presence.

"Eileen," asks the lady, "do you have family?"

I shake my head. If my aunt still lives, I want nothing to do with her.

"Would you like to do some training?" the lady persists. "We can give you a flat in the town to live in. You'll have money of your own if you take a job. What would you like to do?"

A job? Where's the bloody money for the years from working here, I want to scream. But instead I look her in the face, searching for the trickery. Sister Monica is motionless by the door.

The lady's face is composed and she writes on her clipboard. "Tell me what you want, Eileen," she encourages. "There's nothing to be scared of."

"I want to live with Maura," I say.

"Maura?" The lady writes that down.

"My friend here." I stare Sister Monica in the face as I say those words. We're not allowed to form friendships. Her blank face stares back at me, but I can see the wheels turning in her mind.

The lady smiles. "Let's talk to Maura. I think if you are friends, that is a good idea. You can be support for each other as you adjust to your new life."

And it's that easy, although it's taken us over twenty years to reach this point. It's 1988, and Ireland has changed. Maura and I leave together, hand in hand, clasping small suitcases. We've been given some clothes, some money. There's a flat for us in town. Not the town nearby, the bigger town on the river where no one will know where we've come from.

The lady opens a car door. "It's not far," she says. "Soon, you'll be at your new home."

I'm scared. Part of me wants to retreat back inside the convent doors, bury my arms in the laundry sink and scrub away these thoughts of freedom. But then Maura squeezes my fingers and together, we walk down the steps to our new life.

For over 150 years, Ireland placed nearly 30,000 women into the Catholic-run institutions known as "Magdalene Laundries." Originally meant as a way for prostitutes to purge their sin through hard work, the Magdalene Laundries evolved into a convenient solution for families wanting to hide the shame of an unwed pregnancy. Sometimes women sent to the institutions had done no more than behave in a way considered overly flirtatious or wanton, or were wrongly accused of promiscuity. In the laundries, the women were forcibly detained and made to slave in total silence, often up to twelve hours a day, with breaks only for simple meals and prayer. If pregnant, they were bullied into giving up their child. They were often mentally and physically mistreated by the nuns. The only way out was if a family member or a priest would vouch for them—often the very people who had sent them there in the first place. Some women died and were buried in unmarked graves. Others went insane and were removed to mental hospitals. It was not uncommon for a girl to enter in her teenage years and remain until she died.

Ireland's last Magdalene Laundry was closed in 1996.

THE GAME

Elaine Burnes

I held the stick loosely. My right thumb rubbed a flaw in the varnished surface, a crack in the veneer, so I turned it for a better grip and realigned the shaft. The white cue ball, marred by smudges of blue chalk, loomed large in this close view. Steady, I told myself. I used to know how to do this. I knew about angles and spin and strategy. But that was a long time ago. That was in college. This was in a hotel bar in Provincetown. I willed the stick to hit the ball, to ricochet off the bumper, to knock the yellow striped nine into the corner pocket. Stick hit ball. Ball hit bumper. Then nothing. Missed the nine by an inch and the cue ball rolled to a stop against a tight cluster of stripes and solids. At least my opponent would have a difficult shot. She watched, unsmiling, not focused on me but on the layout of the balls on the green felt tabletop. I straightened and shrugged. No excuses.

The silence of my concentration was infiltrated by music drifting from the dance floor downstairs and murmurs from the young women gathered at the bar like wildebeests around a watering hole. Some turned to watch us, a group of kids played air hockey and a foursome shot at the other pool table.

My opponent was a striking woman. That's what had made me challenge her. I wanted to see her bend and reach, to be able to look at her while she concentrated on her shot, unable to look back at me. Tall, solid and confident, she wore her hair cut short on the sides but long on top, with a tantalizing lock draped over her right brow. Flecks of gray added to the allure. She'd been around the block a few times. She knew what she was doing.

She took her game seriously, circling the table, eyeing her options. The sleeves of her denim shirt were rolled to the elbow, exposing lean, muscled forearms. Her shirt tucked into black jeans that fit tight, but well, decorated by a thick, leather belt with a large silver buckle. She leaned over the table. Her hands could easily break the cue stick, I thought, yet she held it gently, her right wrist fluid like a violinist's. Her left hand splayed on the felt bed, thumb and index finger supporting the stick. She wore a ring, but so did I.

She cracked the cue ball into the clustered pack, acknowledging I'd left her in a hole so she just blew it open, changing the game. There is almost nothing so satisfying as the sharp clatter of billiard balls against each other, a crash of sound waves in an otherwise silent game. The colorful orbs skittered across the table, clacking into each other and the cushions. Instant, brief chaos. The Big Bang writ small. Nothing dropped, so it was my turn. She looked at me but her brown eyes, ebony in the dim light of the bar, betrayed no emotion.

A light breeze cooled my back. The double doors to the patio stood open, and the scent of low tide drifted in from the harbor across the street, brine and fish competing with sweat and beer. Dusk deepened as the August sun set over my home back in

Boston. I'm always a little off kilter in P-town, east of a city I think of as being west of nothing but ocean, and a place where I'm suddenly a member of the majority. The game changes in P-town.

I felt her eyes on me as I scoped the table and wished I still had the touch. This time I had options. One easy shot. I leveled the cue, sighted carefully and checked that the stick would glide smoothly through my fingers. I wiped my hand on my jeans to be sure and set up again. The music and the murmurs dropped away. My opponent faded and I was left with the shaft, the cue ball and the nine, again. I called it. Side pocket. This time I hit better. The white ball spun away from me, connected and stopped, transferring its energy to the nine, which rolled smoothly till it vanished. I glanced at her. She gave a nod of acknowledgement. Maybe an exhale. Focus. The next shot would not be so easy. Solids blocked my path leaving me with a banked shot.

When I was good, and I was very good, I'd enter a Zen state. My senses would narrow or expand as needed. Sounds dropped away, lights brightened, focus sharpened. It's not about my opponent. My only opponent is myself.

Pool is high school physics and geometry. Points move across a level plane in straight lines, angles and occasional curves. The angle of incidence equals the angle of reflection. Force equals mass times acceleration. Momentum and inertia, a transfer of kinetic energy. All I have to do is measure the angle and the distance, calculate the force, anticipate the spin, adjust for the friction of my fingers, align the stick. If I do each of these things perfectly, I can't help but sink the ball.

I tried to concentrate but was too aware of her watching me. This time I hit my striped ball, but nothing went in. I'm no longer very good or even good. That takes practice, and I've had other things to focus on. No foul, at least.

Pool is two-dimensional and simple, unlike life, which is three-dimensional and messy, with textures and smells, ups and downs—where success defies easy formulas. Life is a longer game, so I won't know for a while yet if I've made the right choices, called the right shots.

Four young things had wandered over. One wore dreadlocks, though she was white, another had so much hardware stapled to her lips I wondered if she could kiss at all. The other two were entwined around each other like a brown and white candy cane. Hardware stepped forward and placed a pile of quarters on the rail. She didn't look at either of us. She wasn't challenging us. Or me. She just wanted the table. When did that happen? When did I change from being the object of a young woman's attention to a mere obstacle to her enjoyment? Someone she had to wait in line behind instead of wait for.

My opponent prepared her next shot. The bar had vanished behind a wall of wildebeests—some held beers and margaritas and turned to watch the action, others huddled, arms draped across shoulders, mouths mashed together. The music was louder now, the low-toned beat pulsing through the floor, the high notes too weak to penetrate.

She bent over her shot. Muscles in her cheek flexed. I resisted the urge to reach out and trace her fine jawline with my finger. In college, I didn't have to worry about being distracted by my opponents. They were mostly boys. In college, I never considered sex with boys, though I never thought about it with girls either. Science labs took all my time. That game changed long ago. Now, I wouldn't mind transferring a little energy with her. Overcoming inertia. Gathering some momentum. I wondered if she was the type to have an affair. I wondered if I was.

She missed a complicated combination. Chalking my cue bought me some time, but it didn't help. We traded misses for

a few rounds before I finally sank my thirteen. Lucky me. The
background noise grew louder, and the young women paced
impatiently. So what. Each time she squinted to aim, flexed her
fingers on the table then cringed when she missed, a little zing
went through me.

Running a hand through her hair, she eyed the setup. I'd left
her with a good shot. I wanted her to smile—maybe when she
sank the ball. She took her time. She could take as long as she
wanted. I was enjoying the view. She wiped a bead of sweat from
her upper lip. Was the room getting warmer or were we? Then
she leaned in for her shot, setting her hand on the table, taking
aim. She drew back the cue but then straightened and fished a
cell phone out of her pocket, checked the number and took the
call. She murmured a few words into the phone, closed it and
looked at me.

"It's time to go, hon. The twins are ready for their story, and
Ginny has to get to her COLAGE thing."

Sugar. I let out a breath. Ginny is hers from a postcollege
marriage, but for ten years she's been mine, too. Fifteen going
on fifty, she's a peer counselor for Children of Lesbians and
Gays Everywhere. The "thing" she has to get to is their dance
downstairs. She's DJ-ing the last half but had insisted on baby-
sitting so we could have a date. The twins have always been
both of ours. They are five going on five and tilt my world. Just
today they reminded me that race cars made of sand are wicked
awesome and listening to the ocean in a seashell can raise the
hairs on the back of your neck. When did I forget that? The
nubile young things who had migrated over to wait their turn
were clueless.

"Can't we finish the game?" I pleaded.

She looked at the table full of balls, then at me, raising an
eyebrow and smiling. "That might take till morning. I haven't

sunk a ball in the last half hour, and you're not doing much better."

The pile of quarters caught my eye. "Fine. All yours," I said to the next generation. I put my stick in the rack.

She took my hand and pulled me to her. "You're such a good sport." Then she kissed me, light and teasing, but it blew me open.

I grabbed her belt and pulled her closer. "Do that again."

She smiled, her eyes bright with desire. "In front of them?" she said, nodding back to our audience. "Can't you wait? The twins will be asleep in half an hour."

I pulled her tighter to me so I could feel her breasts against mine, her stomach move with each breath. I glanced at the youngsters and winked. I kissed her, deep and serious, swaying our hips to the music and moving my leg between hers. She moaned. The noise dropped away, the lights dimmed.

She pulled back, needing to breathe. "Damn, you're good," she said, her voice low and ragged.

"Watch your language." I slapped her bottom playfully. She threw her head back and laughed.

I sighed and leaned against her. "When will we be able to come to Women's Week instead of Family Week?"

She wrapped her arms around me. "In about, oh, thirteen years, when the twins go off to college. If we can afford it." She took my hand and led me to the stairs.

"Dang, I'll be an old lady by then," I complained.

"But think how much more practice you'll have had."

THE GIFT

Sacchi Green

The desert under the full moon lay still and serene, as though the storms of war and of nature had never swept across it. With a bit of squinting and a dose of wishful thinking, Lou could almost fancy that the pale expanse of sand was a snowfield. But the distant hills to the north and the ice-glazed mountains of the Hindu Kush far beyond weren't the Swiss Alps, and only imagination spurred by loneliness could show Meg, in her trim ski kit, tracing elegant curves across the slopes and throwing up plumes of new powder as she raced by. Or sinking into a hot tub at the end of an exhilarating day, skin flushed by more than the rising steam.

Sand or snow. Made no difference. What mattered was that it was Christmas, and Lou was four time zones away from Meg. No, wait, Switzerland wasn't as far from Afghanistan as their home in England; three time zones. Or three and a half—and how had that half hour bit got stuck in, anyway? Never mind. She tilted her bottle and drank the next-to-last draft of water.

Almost midnight here, just midevening in the Alps. Meg would be at dinner with friends or already partying in one chalet or another. That was as it should be, no matter how much Lou longed to be with her. They'd planned the ski holiday long before Lou's orders had come through, and it was better for Meg to go than to sit alone at home. Except that home was where Lou needed most to envision her. To envision them both, together.

Bugger envisioning! Lou needed to see Meg right now, tonight, if only for a moment. Touching her, hearing her, feeling the brush of her soft hair, the warmth of her breath, the accelerating rhythm of her heart—all these were impossible, and Lou had chosen to accept that, knowing how hard it would be, even knowing how much she was hurting Meg. Seeing her was just as impossible, Lou knew that, and the sooner she forgot about what the old Afghani grandmother had said this morning, the better—mind games, even if the woman hadn't meant it that way.

Even so, Lou slid a hand into the pocket of her camo jacket. The flat brass box was warm to the touch from her own body heat. The gift had been a generous gesture on the old woman's part, too generous, really, when all Lou had done was to bring food from the mess tent to the family group huddled outside the hospital complex.

They'd been there for hours, waiting while the doctors worked on two small children with serious injuries. Bringing them food and water had been the least she could do. She had to confess to some slight curiosity as well; sick or injured children were brought in all too often, but this was the first time a woman had accompanied the men. It was she who had tended the children, and the bearded men had shown her something approaching deference.

The curiosity had been mutual, Lou was sure. The fierce old eyes peering out from the enveloping *burka* had seemed to follow her intently, until, as Lou collected the emptied cups and bowls, rough, wrinkled fingers had pressed the box into her hand. Would refusing a gift be taken as an insult? The woman spoke a few words, and then a nurse came out to lead the family into the post-op tent.

A local civilian maintenance worker had been watching the whole encounter. Lou asked what the woman had said, and after some hesitation he'd translated the words as meaning something along the lines of, "Catch the moon in the box and see your heart's desire." He'd started to add something about how foolish women's tales were, stammered as he remembered that Lou was a woman as well as a soldier and escaped back to his work with relief.

It *was* foolishness, of course. A good story to tell Meg tomorrow in email, but nothing worth dwelling on now. Tonight she'd just have to make do with some more serious envisioning of Meg, and that might be better done in her warm cot, except that tents provided very little in the way of privacy.

Lou raised her water bottle in a toast. "Cheers, sweetheart! Merry Christmas! Have a great time!" She drained the last few trickles of liquid. "Here's hoping yours is a gin and tonic!" Wherever Meg was, she'd be thinking of Lou tonight. And she'd have a g&t in hand. Maybe she was even gazing toward the moon at this very moment, though it might be too low in the sky just now to clear the Alpine peaks.

In Afghanistan the moon soared high overhead, revealing every object, including Lou, with relentless clarity. She shifted uneasily. This perch on sandbags heaped in an angle of the perimeter wall gave her a better view of the desert than was strictly safe, although "safe" was a relative term at best in a world where even a transport lorry full of frozen turkeys for the soldiers' Christmas dinner had been blown up by insurgents. The holiday had still been jolly enough, with more turkeys rushed in by plane, plenty of sweets and packages from home and a great deal of singing and chaffing and merrymaking that got as near to boisterous as the lads could manage without proper drinks.

Lou had joined in with her customary high spirits, but the time came when she needed to get away from the noise and forced cheer. If she couldn't be with Meg, at least she could be alone to think about being with Meg. Now a glance back at the main camp showed row upon row of tents glowing golden with interior light, like a scene from some fantastic Arabian Nights tale.

She turned back to the cold white moonlight and her own thoughts, which reverted, in spite of herself, to the little box. She'd opened it once already, of course, and found a round mirror set inside the lid. When her own face stared back at her, with a bit of her camo shirt showing at her throat, she'd figured, well, close enough. Being here, in uniform, doing her part, *was* truly her heart's desire, surpassed only by Meg's love. The miracle was that Meg, for all her pain at the separation, for all her horror of war—Meg, who was never violent except in her attack on a challenging ski slope or in defense of those she loved—would still let Lou have both.

The box in Lou's hand still felt warm, but it was just too bloody silly to think that there was anything mystical about it. Still, Meg was bound to ask, if Lou told the story, whether she'd tried it by moonlight. So as long as she was here…

Moonlight glinted on tiny mirror chips set into the metal between inlaid ovals of lapis lazuli, while the stones themselves, so vividly blue in the daytime, looked almost black. Merely a trifle, actually, its like could be found in any market in Lashkar Gah or Kandahar, or, for that matter, on many a flea market barrow on Portobello Road in London. Nothing special about it, except, perhaps, the borrowed glamour that moonlight seems to cast on ordinary objects.

Lou's fingers still shook as she fumbled to undo the brass clasp. Just the cold night air, of course. Before lifting the lid all the way she shifted around on the sandbags until the moonlight came over her right shoulder. Then, with a catch in her breath and a touch of defiance, she opened the box all the way and tilted the round mirror to catch the moon directly in its center.

The white orb hung there, clear and sharp. Lou started to breathe again. Then a mist crept across the glass, and the moon's image spread to fill the whole surface. Only condensation, of course, from her own breath. She fumbled with one hand to find a handkerchief to clear it, gave up and was about to try with the elbow of her jacket when the mist began to dissipate on its own until only a few drifting wisps remained. The light, much softer now, still filled the entire mirror.

A blurred scene began to form, or to emerge, as though it came closer, or as though Lou herself moved forward into it. The surroundings were vaguely familiar, but all she could focus on was the figure standing in the center, head bowed, smooth russet hair swinging forward against her cheeks. Lou knew the scent, the softness, of that hair, as well as she knew anything in life. And she knew the feel of the lovely body beneath, exposed entirely to her gaze, as well as she knew her own flesh.

"Meg..." If only she would raise her head! But the figure moved slowly, face still hidden, down a step or two. More tendrils of mist floated around her. "No...don't go..." Meg kept on, sinking gradually downward into something denser than mist, water that lapped about her body until only her head, shoulders and the upper curves of her breasts showed above it. "Meg..."

And then Meg leaned her head back against the edge of the

hot tub and sighed. Lou could hear that sigh inside her own head. And now she could see Meg's face, that particular blend of eyes and nose and lovely lips, of gentleness and strength and elegance, that for Lou would forever define beauty. And love. And home.

There was sadness in Meg's expression and dampness on her cheeks that might have been due to the hot, humid air, or might have included a tear or two. She lifted her head, raised an arm from the water and reached out to a tray beside the tub. Lou hadn't noticed it before, but now she saw the glass and knew beyond question what it contained.

Meg held up the drink. "Cheers, Lou darling! Merry Christmas!" She took a healthy draft of her gin and tonic. Then, more softly, "Keep safe. Please." She drank again, uncharacteristically deeply, and added, "I'm truly proud of you, right where you are. But...oh, I miss you so much!" She emptied the glass, closed her eyes and leaned back, sliding a little lower into the water.

Lou needed to reach out, to brush the tears from Meg's face, even more than she needed to breathe. She felt torn into two separate beings. One clutched a brass box in the cold Afghan desert; one floated through the steam rising from the hot tub and sank into the water so close to Meg that their legs intertwined. As heat rose from her feet all along her body, the colder world retreated, until it was just the faintest of memories.

Lou couldn't make her voice work, but her fingertips could feel the curve of Meg's cheek, and throat, and shoulder. Meg sighed. Her face relaxed, and her lips curved into a smile. "I can almost feel you here with me," she murmured, eyes still closed. "Are you thinking of me now, sweetheart?"

"Thinking" didn't come close to describing it, for either of them. Meg seemed not to find it strange that her arms could go around Lou and Lou's around her. They clung to each other, moving gently together in the slow swirl of the water, bathed in a warm current of love and joy. No dream could ever be sweeter, Lou felt—until Meg opened her eyes and looked directly into Lou's. "I can even see you, darling!" Meg's voice held more delight than surprise. "How lovely!"

That was the sweetest moment of all. And even when Lou felt the pull of that half of herself left behind in the desert and knew that she was drifting away, not from Meg, but merely from that particular time and place, she held the image of Meg's loving smile in her heart.

The night was dark again. Lou still held the box, but the moon was so low in the sky that only a sliver of it still showed in the mirror. Tilting the lid brought the bright disc back into its center but accomplished nothing further. Lou drew a deep breath, rose slowly from the sandbags and started back across the compound toward the clustered tents. In spite of the cold air, warmth still suffused her body, lingering until her bed could capture and preserve it.

She was too tired and too much at peace to try to analyze what had happened, except for a fleeting thought about what she should tell Meg. Or, perhaps, what she should ask. Just a humorous tale about the old Afghan woman and a joke about an "envisioning aid" and a light account of her "dream" might be the best course.

It was midmorning before Lou had time to write even a brief email, and by then Meg had beat her to it. *Dearest Lou*, Meg wrote. *The strangest thing happened last night! It was like the most marvelous Christmas gift! I was in the hot tub in the chalet, thinking of you, and...well, maybe it was just that drinking a g&t in all that heat made me lightheaded—I should know better—but I can't believe it. I don't want to believe it. Please don't laugh. Just tell me where you were last night, and whether you were thinking of me.*

Lou felt warm all over again, and a bit light-headed herself. *You tell me yours and then I'll tell you mine,* she typed. *It's a long story, and I only have a minute now, but if there's any laughing to be done, we'll do it together. Always.*

ROCK PALACE

Miel Rose

'd been contemplating the pros and cons of taking Lilly to visit the farm for some time. It was one of those decisions where the outcome could make or break a thing, and it took a while for me to stop shying away from the risk. It was halfway through June before I faced those fears and saw waiting wasn't doing me a bit of good.

I had spent huge chunks of my childhood on that farm, raised by my grandma. She was still strong as an ox, but she was getting up there in age. It had been years since small farms had made much of a living in those parts. She had downscaled and sold what remained of the dairy cows her folks had tended decades before, all but a couple of sweet-tempered jerseys. She had a small nest egg, and mostly she farmed for herself, plus family and immediate neighbors.

She liked to take vacations every now and then, usually into town to stay with my aunt. Take a break from tending the goats and chickens, cows and vegetables. She had a promise from me that I would keep the farm running when she was gone (both when she was in town and when she "finally passed over," as she put it). It was a promise I meant to keep.

Gram would be taking off this particular weekend to see a play she had tickets for, and I'd be watching the farm. I wanted to take Lilly out there with me, which wasn't a move I'd usually make while courting a girl.

Most of my life I had been simultaneously proud and ashamed of where I come from. When your identities are many, you often feel stranded in the middle of a busy intersection, not knowing which way to take to find your home. Sometimes you pick one at the expense of the others in order to find a place to fit in, a community. My queerness had taken precedence awhile back, which did not change the fact that I was rural and poor, living in the city. I was surrounded by downwardly mobile queers from the suburbs, and I passed as one of them. This was leaving other parts of me feeling lonely and invisible.

You leave the place you were raised and sometimes you leave your context. I had tried to build myself another one, but it was full of holes, a sinking ship. Having just turned thirty, I was feeling that post–Saturn return urge to cut through the bullshit, clarify who my people were and get down to the business of following my heart and my gut. Just fucking do it.

I was tired of renting, tired of slumlords and shitty apart- ments that I worked so hard to make decent while paying someone else's mortgage. I wanted to settle, and I wanted to find folks who wanted to settle with me. Among them, I was hoping to find a girl to cuddle up against on those brutal winter nights when the walls of the old farmhouse felt like they were made of tissue paper.

For years, I had made it a habit of falling for high femmes who tended to scream at the sight of insects, didn't own shoes that would hold up on gravel and only liked getting dirty in the bedroom. These women were strong, brilliant people, but there were always parts of my life I just could not share with them.

Lilly was different. Being also from a rural, working background she made me feel at home in a way I hadn't even realized I'd been missing until I met her. It stirred things up, got me thinking about the slow building pressure I'd been sensing in my life. She was like vinegar, my thoughts the baking soda, turning the inside of my brain into the volcano in a sixth grader's science fair project.

She was sweet and grounded and shockingly honest. She had sharp insight and more energy than anyone I had ever met. She laughed at me even when I wasn't trying to be funny and instead of feeling embarrassed about this, I felt strangely proud.

This lingering apprehension was silly, but I couldn't seem to shake it. The farm had always been a safe haven for me, and I protected it like my heart.

She seemed genuinely excited though, when I asked her to go out there with me.

"Taylor! I love goats! I always wanted some growing up, but my parents never went for it. Can I milk them?" She bubbled over, throwing her arms around me and pressing herself against me in a way that made me frantic.

Lilly was almost as tall as my five feet ten with a body that was made up of one luscious curve after another. Awe inspiring. She was a big girl and she was not ashamed of it. I embarrassed myself regularly comparing her to certain divinity in my head.

"Sure, sweets, you can have your pick of farm chores," I said, wrapping my arms around her waist and burying my nose in her brown curls. Anything, this girl could have anything she wanted from me.

* * *

The summer had started off hot that year, and the cutoff jean shorts Lilly was wearing when I picked her up were going to drive me crazy all day. She was carrying a bag with knitting needles sticking out the top. She always brought some kind of project with her wherever she went, to keep her hands busy.

"I'm wearing the bikini I knit last week under this, so I hope you have a swimming hole somewhere on this farm."

I swallowed convulsively. "You bet, sugar. There's a great one not too far from the house."

She grabbed her needles and started knitting as I drove away. "I brought sandwiches if you're hungry. Cheese and sprouts."

Lilly was raised by hippies. The sandwiches were probably made on home-baked whole wheat bread. I was raised on bologna and white bread with my dad, but had been spoiled by my grandma's complex and nutritious food.

The farm was about an hour from Lilly's house. I tried to keep my mind on the road and the pleasant conversation Lilly was trying to make. I tried to stop staring at the swell of her breasts exposed by the low cut of her tank top, something I couldn't help but notice every time I glanced over at her. This was going to come to a head soon; that was obvious. The realization filled me with a restless tension and made the floor of my stomach drop about two feet.

It hadn't rained in the last week and the final stretch of dirt road was dry, so we had to roll up the windows to block out clouds of dust. The air was hot and heavy with humidity. We were both sticky with sweat, our skin gritty by the time we pulled up to the farmhouse.

Lilly jumped out of the truck right away, a look of awe on her beautiful face. Turning to me she said, "Taylor, it's gorgeous! You didn't tell me."

I'll admit, early summer is a good time on the farm. Something about the light and the new green of everything, all the imperfections of the old buildings get smoothed out. The flowerbeds and the vegetable gardens haven't been completely taken over by weeds yet. The grass is still pretty low. Come back in August, and this place is a fucking jungle.

It had been my home for much of my life and would be again. I put as much of my energy and heart into it as I could manage with my busy days. I loved it like no other place, but I hadn't thought to describe it to this girl as beautiful. I was so deeply gratified by her admiration, it just shed more light on how anxious I'd been about her reaction to the place.

I grinned at her, letting my heart loosen up in a different way. I filled with relief as that tight place eased inside me.

She grinned back at me, closed the distance between us and placed her lips on my dusty cheek. I took a deep breath and reminded myself that it's never good to rush these things. We had two whole days together out here, alone. I didn't have to fuck this girl in the driveway five minutes into our stay.

I brushed some stray hair behind her ear and said, "You really like it, princess?"

"I love it. It feels amazing here." She looked over her shoulder at the house and I leaned in, kissed the hollow between her neck and jaw. I allowed myself that much.

I cleared the dust and tension from my throat and said, "Lilly, you want to catch that swim now? There's really nothing for us to do until dusk, unless you want to weed Gram's perennial beds."

She giggled, ran her fingers over the back of my neck, and turned eyes on me in a way that made my center melt like butter on a griddle. She said, "I'd love to go for a swim."

* * *

The path to the swimming hole had been cleared recently. I hadn't gotten around to it this year, so I figured maybe my aunt's husband had been out here. He was a good guy and tried to help Gram out as much as he had time for.

It wasn't far to the river, but our sweat was running freely by the time we reached the bend that formed a pool just big enough for a satisfying dip. I started stripping off my jeans and T-shirt, feeling self-conscious despite the boxer briefs and tank top I had on underneath. Lilly, on the other hand, couldn't get out of her clothes fast enough, and the bikini she wore was just a little bit more than a formality. She strode into the water, yelped at the cold, and dunked under at the deepest point. I followed more slowly, letting myself acclimate. She swam circles around me like a selkie, giggling and splashing at me until I dove at her, pulling her underwater with me. We surfaced, sputtering.

Her arms wrapped around me, pressing her warm mammalian body to mine in the cold water. She smelled so good, with traces of vanilla, river water and summer skin. I wanted to lay her down, stretch her out and touch all that exposed flesh.

I remembered a place I used to hide as a kid, a place of rock and sky and soft mosses. I had spent a lot of my turbulent adolescence hiding out there, reading sci-fi novels, thinking, crying when shit got bad. I learned to jerk off there, reading old smutty paperbacks I had found in my dad's garage. The give of the moss under my ass and the rock rough against my back created an intense and irresistible contrast. It was my palace, my fortress, whatever I needed. I had never even thought of sharing that spot with anyone.

"I want to take you someplace," I said, angling our bodies toward land.

I watched her pull herself out of the water, watched her body rejoin gravity, that awkward moment of heavy disorientation. Her bikini bottoms sagged around her curves, saturated with water, and she pulled at them, giggling self-consciously.

"I haven't quite figured that part out yet," she said, smiling back at me in this way I felt in my gut.

The opening to my old hideout looked dank and cramped and shadowed in a way that embarrassed me and made me wonder what had possessed me to bring a girl here.

"I haven't been here in a while; maybe we should forget it," I said, scratching the back of my head.

"It's through here?" Her voice was excited, up for anything. She got down on her hands and knees and started wiggling through the opening. My face heated up watching her from behind, her ass so sexy, her back arched to crawl through the small space in the rock. I worried about her knees. In five seconds she was out of sight, just her toes visible in the dappled sunlight on the other side.

"Holy shit, this is beautiful!"

I was way smaller the last time I had come here, but I crouched down and crawled through, the rock hard and rough under my weight.

The space opened up, a small chamber carpeted in soft, thick moss. The walls were formed by massive granite boulders, smoothed down and spit out by long-ago glaciers, clustering together against the hill to hide this space, an old, secret privacy. The sky was an intense blue above us, with small shreds of sunlight filtering down through the trees on the hillside. She was staring around in wonder, her knees pressing into the damp, moss-covered earth. She sat down, arranging herself, and looked over at me.

"So, how many girls have you brought here?" she asked, her

head cocked, smiling in this way that said she was a good sport but I'd better be careful about answering.

"I've never brought a girl here," I said. "The girls I've dated are too city to appreciate this."

She looked away, her face a shutter slowly closing.

"I'm not really your type, am I," she said, like she was sad, but also resigned.

I was baffled. I looked at her, her body so ripe and luscious that her handmade bikini didn't even begin to contain it. I felt a pain in my heart, a hairline fracture, watching this girl lose her confidence. She was sitting there in a swimsuit she had been taught her whole life she did not have a right to wear, and she looked so fucking beautiful I thought I might hyperventilate or dissolve if I didn't get my hands on her soon. How could she possibly not be aware of her effect on me?

"You are exactly my type. I've just never met anyone like you before."

She looked at me, curiously. "Ditto," she said, and I laughed, because that's always what the emotionally stunted guy says in the movies after the girl says, "I love you."

"No, I mean it," she said. "That's kind of how I feel about you too."

She was serious. I saw it in the crease forming on her brow.

"Come here," she said. All her insecurity gone, her body opened up like an invitation.

Her feet were closest to me so I went for those first, raised her toes to my lips. Her giggles turned to a low moan as I ran my tongue over her instep.

"Taylor, come *here*."

She grabbed me and, lying back, pulled me to her; waterlogged clothing pressed between us. Her mouth found mine and I couldn't remember ever feeling anything more soft than my bottom lip between hers, her skin under my hands or her body pressed underneath me.

It was the easiest thing in the world to slip her breasts from her bikini top, slip her nipple into my mouth. She was so generous with her response, with her body. It made my heart ache in my chest the way she opened herself to me, gave me access. It made me painfully hard the way her body moved in waves under me. The way she sighed and moaned, arched her back, cried out when my teeth found her neck.

I wanted to please her until there was no question in her mind that she was a goddess, no question that she deserved every second of pleasure I could give her. The beast in me wanted to get rough with her, sink my teeth into that luscious flesh and watch the colors bloom under her skin. I wanted to mark her, make her irrevocably mine.

Words fell from our mouths in clusters between kisses.

You feel so good. I've wanted this for so long. I love your body, you are so fucking beautiful. I love the weight of you on top of me. Yes, please, just like that, yes.

It felt ridiculously good to hear the word *baby* come out of her mouth, all soft and rolling off her tongue, and know she was talking to me. It felt ridiculously good to slip my fingers between her legs and into all that hot wetness, watching her eyes roll back and her limbs go weak as I slid in and out of her. I found a spot inside her and when I stroked it at the right angle the most glorious sounds came out of her mouth. I wanted to make her come with a fierceness that surprised me, made all my muscles tense and my teeth close on her neck a bit harder than I meant to.

With a sharp cry, she convulsed around my fingers, spurts of her come splashing her thighs and soaking into the moss. I kissed away the pain I had caused, held her until the convulsions stopped and she came back to herself. Slowly she opened her eyes and looked into mine, the light and shadow from the leaves above playing on her beautiful face.

"I'm so glad it's you," she mumbled and pulled my lips down to hers.

Even with all the heat our bodies generated, the combination of the lengthening shadows and our wet clothing had us shivering and covered in gooseflesh before long. We crawled from our hideaway searching for some afternoon sun. We found a nice patch stretching across the bed in the guest room and discovered just how squeaky one of those old brass bed frames can be. I am truly surprised we didn't break the thing—and that we haven't since.

It was dark before we dragged ourselves to the kitchen, starving. Lilly was adorable in one of my button-ups, only the middle two buttons fastened, the fabric straining against the gorgeous abundance of her chest.

There was all the expected awkwardness of sharing a kitchen for the first time with someone you are newly in love with. Despite the fact that the kitchen is large, with plenty of counter space, I couldn't seem to be anywhere but right on top of her. We were light-headed from sex hormones and lack of food, and we could barely keep our hands off each other long enough to produce anything edible. Finally Lilly kicked me out to go milk the goats and, in the absence of my distractions, conjured up some culinary magic.

Eating that first meal together, I remember wondering how each bite of food could possibly make it past the swollen mass my heart had become, and how the hell I was going to convince this woman to marry me and start some crazy family with me in a falling-down farmhouse in the middle of nowhere.

It was a lot easier than I expected, but that's another story.

WHEN HEARTS RUN FREE

Radclyffe writing
as L. L. Raand

I'd only been a Were for a few weeks, but I knew I shouldn't even be looking at the Alpha of the Adirondack lupus pack, let alone lusting after her. Then again, I'd never been very good at following protocol—probably if I had, I wouldn't have found myself in a moonlit clearing deep in the mountains of Upstate New York about to undergo my first fully conscious shift. If I'd been following the rules, I probably wouldn't have tried to sedate the teenager in the throes of Werefever either, but by the time the police had found her in an alley she was so far gone she was seizing. She was going to die without treatment, and there wasn't time to wait for the Were medic on call to get to the ER. As it turned out, I was too late, and the girl died. But not before she bit me.

I don't remember much of what happened after her teeth sank into my wrist like two rows of razor blades, sharp and bright. Even when the flesh tore and my instruments slipped through my fingers on a river of red, I didn't feel the pain. The burn came later, at the same time as the fever. Then the dreams. Fragments of images flickered through my rioting brain, scattered patches of light and dark like broken bits of sunshine littered over the forest floor—chasing me while I ran, the hunter and the hunted. My muscles screamed, my bones shattered and in the back of my mind always the low, throaty growl urging me to run. Run. *Run.*

When I woke, my head was clear, my stomach hollow with hunger and everything was different. Beyond the closed door of my hospital room, I heard the staff conversing at the nurses' station at the other end of the hall as clearly as if they were standing beside my bed. I gasped and instantly gagged on the miasma of hospital smells deluging me—cafeteria food, antiseptic, disease, the living and the dead.

"Breathe slowly through your mouth. It will help," a voice as rich and lush as dark chocolate said from somewhere in the shadows of my room. "After a while you'll learn to filter out the sounds and smells, when you want to."

"What happened?" My memory was still patchy.

A blonde appeared beside my bed. She was about my age, late twenties or early thirties and a few inches above average, putting her near my height. Lithe and on the muscular side of lean, wearing a faded green T-shirt tucked into blue jeans. Beneath the smooth skin of her exposed arms the muscles were etched and taut. "You were turned four days ago by an insurgi, a rogue Were. A wolf Were."

"A wolf Were," I said, a statement more than a question. She nodded. "You?"

"Born and bred," she said with a hint of a grin. "My name is Sylvan. Your sponsor, Roger, will be by later. He'll help you through the transition."

"So, what's next?" I pushed myself up in bed and took stock.

For someone whose system had just undergone a violent, rapid mutation at the genetic, subcellular level, I felt pretty damn good. In fact, I felt terrific. I was hungry. And I was horny. I breathed deeply and smelled female. I took another look at the blonde, noting the thrust of her small breasts beneath the green cotton, the smooth, flat plane of her abdomen, the gentle flare of her hips, the tight length of her thighs. The hunger in my belly moved lower, mutated like my cells into something fierce and untamed.

"Should I breathe slowly through my mouth now, too?" I barely contained the urge to vault over the short metal railing on the side of my bed and take her to the floor.

"That probably won't help." She didn't move back but held my gaze steadily. "You're not human anymore. What you're feeling right now is perfectly normal for a wolf."

"How many female wolves want to mate with other females?"

A growl came from the other side of the room, and I realized we weren't alone. Somehow I knew it was a bodyguard. A gravelly voice murmured, "Alpha," with a warning note.

I sniffed and smelled male, and my vision hazed with red. I shuddered, my spine tingling, my vocal cords quivering with a barely audible snarl.

"Alpha, please. This is not advisable," the male said, more urgently this time.

Sylvan waved her hand as if to silence the cautionary voice and grinned again. The rims of her irises narrowed into a deep indigo band around flat black pupils. Her breasts rose and fell faster beneath her T-shirt. "More females than you might think."

"That's good to know." I clenched my fists, fighting to hold still, to force down the flames that scorched me from the inside out. Dimly, I registered a different kind of burning sensation in my palms, and when I glanced down, saw that my fingernails had elongated into short, curved dark claws. My hands bled from a series of crescent lacerations, but I felt no pain. Only want. "I think maybe you should leave. Something's happening to me." I sucked in a shaky breath. "I think I might be dangerous."

"You can't hurt me," she whispered, leaning over me now. Close, too close. Her scent, a mix of burning autumn leaves cut through with cinnamon and sweet clover, grew heavier, darker. "It's your wolf. She wants to be free."

I panted, twisting beneath the sheets. "I think I might…Jesus, I want—"

"But it's too soon for you to control her." She straightened and drifted back into the shadows. The pressure in my chest eased a fraction. "You'll learn. You have two weeks until the next full moon. Welcome to the Adirondack Timberwolf pack, whelp."

I hadn't seen her again, but I thought of her every spare minute when I wasn't being poked, prodded and psychoanalyzed by the human physicians or being poked, prodded and indoctrinated into Were society by my sponsor. Her scent lingered like a haunting refrain, keeping me always on edge.

Tonight the moon was full.

"Ready?" Roger asked as the moon climbed to its zenith.

"Sure," I said. I wasn't. I hadn't had nearly enough time to adjust to the physical changes, let alone incorporate all the hierarchical social rules of the pack. But instinctively I knew that any show of weakness would be a mistake. I felt like I was coming out of my skin, and I guess I was.

I tried to appear casual as I followed Roger toward the Pack. Maybe thirty or forty males and females gathered beneath the trees, milling restlessly in the slanting shafts of silvery moonlight. All of them moved with the powerful glide of predators. Some were already nude, others in the process of undressing.

"*Mutia,*" a statuesque redhead growled as I passed.

Mutt. To the *regii*, the purebreds—the natural-born Weres—I was less than a second-class citizen, I was a genetic blight. The US Order of Were Affairs had agreed to sponsor, i.e., indoctrinate, any human turned accidentally, but not everyone in the Were population was happy about being forced to accept "genetic inferiors."

I was a physician. I knew I wasn't inferior, not on any level. Once the mutation was complete, I was physiologically no different than any other lupus Were. Once trained, I would be able to shift at will, and I was already as fast, as strong and potentially as deadly as any other lupus female my size. Maybe more so—before my turning, I'd been a trained martial artist. I could fight. I loved competitive sparring. I loved winning.

I could have told the Pack bitches who saw me as a threat that they had no worries, because I had no designs on their studs. None whatsoever. But I wasn't going to crawl on my belly to be accepted or to avoid a fight. I hadn't been at the bottom of the pack, any pack, since I was an intern a decade ago, so keeping my gaze down when the redheaded bitch challenged me, as Roger had instructed I do when the situation arose, took all my self-discipline. The tiny hairs on the back of my neck stood up, and I couldn't completely suppress the growl that resonated in my throat. She snarled and took a step closer, and if I hadn't caught a flicker of gold in the moonlight and seen her just at that moment, I probably would've done something stupid—like answered the bitch's challenge right then and there and gotten my ass chewed up. Literally.

Sylvan, a phalanx of Weres behind her, stalked out of the woods into the clearing. She wore skintight black jeans and nothing else. Her breasts rode high and proud, the muscles in her chest and abdomen rippling seductively beneath moon-kissed skin. I could smell her across the clearing, her scent so heady my mouth literally watered. My sex tightened and desire choked my senses.

"Sylvan." I whispered, but a whisper among Weres might as well have been a shout.

Utter silence fell over the Pack.

"No!" Roger gripped my arm, but it was too late.

She was all I could see, all I could smell, all I could sense, and I took a step forward, my eyes fixed on her face. I barely registered the slash of silver before my legs were cut out from under me and I fell hard, face first to the forest floor. The weight on my back crushed me into the rich loam, and I tasted blood where a tooth had cut my lip. A knee in the center of my back kept me pinned, and one iron-tight thigh rested alongside my hip. An arm bar on the back of my neck prevented me from raising my head, but I didn't need to see. I could scent her, sense her, feel her heat—some part of me beyond words, beyond thought, knew her.

"You forget yourself, whelp," Sylvan rasped in my ear.

I'd worn only a T-shirt and sweatpants in preparation for shifting, and I felt the hard points of her nipples against my shoulder blades as she leaned close. Flame surged from deep in my core and poured into my chest, driving my breath out on a moan.

"I'm sorry, Alpha. I'm sorry," I gasped, suddenly burning up. A soul-deep ache tore my muscle from bone, shattering my mind. A thousand knives scored my skin, flaying sanity along with my flesh. "I...oh, god...I can't breathe...hurts..."

"You'll be all right," Sylvan whispered, her mouth soft against my ear. "Let her come." Then she rolled away, calling, "Roger!"

I screamed. My world disintegrated in a fury of agony, and all I had to cling to was her scent, her voice, the weight of her flesh on my flesh. When I came into myself once more, I was surrounded by wolves. I shook my head, took a step, and fell. A nose nuzzled my neck, as if urging me to rise. I focused on the black muzzle and large dark eyes of the hovering wolf and recognized Roger's scent. He lifted his lip in a wolfy smile, and I tried another step. Then another. I felt powerful in a way I never had before, my body and mind intimately attuned. I laughed and heard myself growl. Roger shouldered me forward. He was bigger than me, longer and taller, but glancing around, I realized that I was bigger than most of the females and some of the males. I stumbled again when I saw her, and this time, I kept my head down, stealing glances when no one was looking.

She was almost pure silver with only a few fingers of black in her thick ruff and along the ridge of her powerful back. Larger than almost all the wolves in the Pack, she stalked the clearing, nosing some, growling at others, playfully nipping a few. I trembled as she drew near, but I did not drop my tail or my head as many others had done. I kept my head lower than hers, but I could not take my eyes away. She was too beautiful.

She was the Pack Alpha, the leader of hundreds of Weres, not just when they were in pelt, but in every aspect of their lives. She led not simply by might, but also by intelligence. She commanded loyalty and was given it, because she was trusted, and because she had earned it. She was my Alpha, just as I was her wolf, and even though I was there not by divinity, but by accident, I felt like I was hers.

Then with a flurry of snapping teeth and rumbling growls, she struck. And though I had never yielded in a battle, never run from a challenge, I did not fight back. Within seconds, I was on my back, her legs straddling my exposed underbelly, her teeth buried in the thick fur of my neck. I tilted my head back and gave her my throat, a soft whine escaping me. Her scent was overpowering now, enveloping me, drowning me, and still the fire inside me burned. She snarled, my throat in her jaws, and shook her head from side to side, reminding me, reminding every wolf within sight or hearing, who ruled the Adirondack Pack. Then she released her viselike grip on me, and I instinctively licked her face. Her wolf-gold eyes gleamed in the moonlight, and for just an instant, her chest and belly settled onto mine. Then she vaulted off, loped into the center of the clearing, raised her head to the moon and howled.

Dozens of voices answered, and my heart stirred, my soul singing with them. I jumped up, shook myself and answered her call. Then we were running, legs pounding, muscles stretching, hearts pumping. The Pack broke into the forest and although I couldn't see her, I knew where she was, just as I knew how to decipher the sounds and scents of the forest. I followed her trail along with a few others, joyfully, freely, with no sense of time, no beginning, no end. Only the thrill of the hunt and the feel of her ahead, calling me. I don't how long I ran or how far, but I gradually became aware of the silence descending upon me. I caught a glimpse of silver slipping between the trees and realized that she and I had outrun the Pack. We were alone in the forest. I slowed and cautiously padded forward into a small clearing. She appeared like a whisper of smoke and I halted, waiting.

She circled me, sniffed me, bumped her shoulder against mine. I waited still, shivering not from exhaustion, but excitement. She rose and set her chest on my shoulders, telling me my place—beneath her. I trembled under her weight, my heart pounding. Her hot breath teased my ear and I rumbled in pleasure. With a powerful thrust of her haunches, she dismounted and, gently setting her muzzle on top of mine, rubbed it back and forth. Then she dipped her head but not her gaze. She would never lower her gaze to anyone—Were or human. Tentatively, I stroked the underside of my jaw over her nose. She allowed the contact only for a few seconds before backing away. Then she turned and raced toward the forest, glancing once over her shoulder, one ear flickering. An invitation. This time when I rushed to follow, she slowed until I ran by her side, and together we hunted.

When the moon slipped down and the night edged toward dawn, she led me to a shelter of fallen pines. She rested her head on her forelegs, studying me solemnly as I curled up by her side. Carefully, cautiously, I edged closer. When she didn't move away, I settled my head on her shoulder. She arched her neck over my back, and together we slept.

"I need to leave," Sylvan murmured, "before the pack sees us."

I'd awakened with nude women I barely knew before, but never on a soft bed of pine needles beneath a crystal sky. And never had I fit so perfectly with anyone. I lay on my back with her head on my shoulder. Her hand rested in the center of my chest, her thigh over mine. I stroked her shoulder.

"How many rules are we breaking?"

"Too many for me to count." Sylvan pushed away and sat up, running her hands through her hair. "Can you find your way back?"

"I'll follow you."

She raised an eyebrow.

"I can smell you." I ran my hand over my chest, down the center of my abdomen, and watched her eyes follow the motion. They were blue again, rimmed in gold, and I remembered her wolf shimmering in the moonlight, a great shining beast. "Every-where I go, I carry you on my skin."

Her face was completely expressionless. "Don't let anyone hear you say that."

I sat up, my skin still warm where she'd lain against me. "Is there an alpha male in the wings? Is that the problem?"

"That's not for you to know." She stood quickly, her jaw set, the word whelp hanging unspoken in the air.

"I know I have a lot to lear—"

"Yes, you have a lot to learn." She stared down at me. "And a place to earn. You'll be challenged."

"Why?" I rose and took a step toward her, watching her muscles harden as she reacted to the threat of me in her space. I shook my head. "I'm not challenging you." I dipped my head and said softly, "Alpha."

"You're not submissive. You're not Wereborn, and…"

"And what?" I feathered my fingers over her cheek and she let me touch her for a few seconds before she edged back, a tight frown eclipsing the brief tenderness I'd glimpsed.

"And you carry my scent," she said sharply.

"Why? Why do I?"

She shook her head. "I don't know. But…" She gestured to the ground where the faint indentations of our bodies lingered. "This can't happen again."

I was powerless. I wasn't even capable of shifting at will yet. She could tear me apart if she wanted, and she would be well within her right. The Pack would demand it if they knew I'd dared touch her. But I didn't care. I crossed the distance she'd put between us, cradled her face in my hands and kissed her. After a heartbeat, her lips parted and her tongue swept over mine, hungry and unhesitant. She flooded me with her wild scent, her raw power, her hidden tenderness. I felt her call in my deepest reaches, and I moaned, aching to answer. She grasped my wrists, forced my arms down and broke away.

"This can never happen again," she repeated, her voice hoarse.

I touched my chest, over my heart. "I am your wolf to command, Alpha. But you cannot rule what I carry in here."

I watched her race toward the trees, as graceful and strong in human form as wolf. There would be other nights, other hunts. Until then I would carry her on my skin, in my senses, in every part of me. I would find her again, when our hearts ran free.

ABOUT THE
AUTHORS

CHEYENNE BLUE (cheyenneblue.com) was born too late to be a hippie and is happiest when writing or traveling. Her erotica has appeared in *Best Women's Erotica, Mammoth Best New Erotica, Best Lesbian Erotica, Best Lesbian Romance* and many other sites. After many years in Ireland, she is now living in Australia.

REBECCA S. BUCK hails from Nottingham, England, but has spent a lot of her time in Slovenia in the former Yugoslavia. Her first novel, *Truths*, was published in 2010 and her second, *Ghosts of Winter*, in 2011.

ELAINE BURNES lives in Massachusetts where, after years of writing and editing nonfiction, she became sick of reality and turned to fiction. She has published numerous short stories, including "The Perfect Gift" in *Skull and Crossbones*, a pirate anthology.

RACHEL KRAMER BUSSEL (rachelkramerbussel.com) is an author, editor and blogger. She hosts In the Flesh Reading Series and has edited over thirty anthologies, including *Orgasmic, Passion, Fast Girls, Spanked, Bottoms Up* and *Do Not Disturb.* She teaches erotic writing workshops nationwide and covers sex, dating, books and pop culture for numerous publications.

MERINA CANYON began writing stories when she was six years old and much later earned an MFA in fiction. Her stories have appeared in *Best Lesbian Love Stories, Sinister Wisdom* and Fraglit.com.

Want to read more by **ANDREA DALE** (cyvarwydd.com)? Check out *Fairy Tale Lust, Sweet Love* and *The Sweetest Kiss,* among others. When not writing, she's a world traveler who hopes to visit Hawaii soon for a third time.

CHARLOTTE DARE's (myspace.com/charlotte_dare) fiction has appeared in *Lesbian Cowboys; Where the Girls Are: Urban Lesbian Erotica; Girl Crazy; Island Girls; Wetter; Purple Panties; Ultimate Lesbian Erotica 2008* & *2009* and *Tales of Travel-rotica for Lesbians Vol. 2.*

CLIFFORD HENDERSON (cliffordhenderson.net) lives and plays in Santa Cruz, California, where she runs The Fun Institute, a school of improv and solo performance, with her partner of eighteen years. Her novels include *ForeWord Review* Book of the Year gold medalist *The Middle of Somewhere.*

THEDA HUDSON is a writer and spiritual advisor/teacher living in Colorado with two semiferal cats, two thousand books and a Mary Poppins outfit complete with a big toy bag that she's not afraid to use. She likes her writing to share the things women don't usually get to talk about.

SACCHI GREEN is based in western Massachusetts, but she does get around. She has contributed to dozens of publications, generally of the erotic persuasion, and has edited/coedited six anthologies herself, most recently *Girl Crazy* and Lambda Literary Award–winner *Lesbian Cowboys.*

CATHERINE LUNDOFF (visi.com/~clundoff) is the author of *Crave: Tales of Lust, Love and Longing* and *Night's Kiss: Lesbian Erotica* and editor of *Haunted Hearths and Sapphic Shades: Lesbian Ghost Stories.* She teaches writing classes at The Loft Literary Center.

ANNA MEADOWS's latest work appeared in *Best Lesbian Romance 2010.* She is a part-time executive assistant, part-time lesbian housewife and a volunteer for the No on 8, Equality for All campaign and for ONE National Gay and Lesbian Archives.

COLETTE MOODY gets turned on by classic movies, witty banter, politics and women with big sexy brains. She has written two historical novels, including the Lambda Literary Award–winner *The Sublime and Spirited Voyage of Original Sin* and *The Seduction of Moxie.*

L. L. RAAND (llraand.com) writes the paranormal romance series, The Midnight Hunters (Book One: *The Midnight Hunt*). Writing as Radclyffe, she has selections in *Best Lesbian Erotica 2006–09,* and her solo erotica collection *Radical Encounters* is a 2010 IPPY silver medalist.

MIEL ROSE is a fierce, rural, low-income, high-intensity queer femme bombshell, just for starters. Her porn stories have appeared in *Best Women's Erotica 2008*, *Best Lesbian Erotica 2008*, *Best Lesbian Love Stories 2009* and *Ultimate Lesbian Erotica 2009*, and she has published a personal essay on femme identity in *Visible: a Femmethology Vol.1*.

JAMIE SCHAFFNER is a 2009 Kirkwood Award finalist and has studied at the UCLA Writers' Program. *Get the Girl* is an excerpt from the novel of the same name. She lives in Los Angeles with her wife.

KATHLEEN WARNOCK's work has previously appeared in several volumes of *Best Lesbian Erotica*, *A Woman's Touch* and *Friction 7*. Kathleen edits books in the near–New York City area by day and has appeared onstage in Ed Valentine's play, *Women Behind the Bush*.

ABOUT
THE EDITOR

RADCLYFFE is a retired surgeon, award-winning author, and publisher with over thirty-five novels and anthologies in print. Seven of her works have been Lambda Literary Award finalists including the Lambda Literary Award winners *Erotic Interludes 2: Stolen Moments* edited with Stacia Seaman; *In Deep Waters 2* and the romance *Distant Shores, Silent Thunder*. In addition to editing *Best Lesbian Romance 2009–11* (Cleis Press), she has edited *Erotic Interludes 2–5* and *Romantic Interludes 1* and *2* with Stacia Seaman (Bold Strokes Books). Her solo erotica collection *Radical Encounters* and her romance *Secrets in the Stone* are 2010 IPPY silver medalists. *Secrets in the Stone* (an RWA Prism Award winner), the intrigue *Justice for All*, and her short-fiction anthology *Romantic Interludes 2* are all 2010 *ForeWord Review* Book of the Year finalists. As L. L. Raand she writes the paranormal romance series *The Midnight Hunters* (Book One: *The Midnight Hunt*). She has selections in multiple anthologies including *Best Lesbian Erotica 2006–9*, is the recipient of the 2003 and 2004 Alice B. Readers' award for her body of work and is a member of the Saints and Sinners Literary Hall of Fame.